W9-BSQ-872

THE MARRIAGE MARKET

BY

LEIGH MICHAELS

MILLS & BOON®

All the characters in this book have no existence outside
the imagination of the author, and have no relation
whatsoever to anyone bearing the same name or names.
They are not even distantly inspired by any individual
known or unknown to the author, and all the incidents
are pure invention.

All Rights Reserved including the right of reproduction
in whole or in part in any form. This edition is published
by arrangement with Harlequin Enterprises II B.V. The
text of this publication or any part thereof may not be
reproduced or transmitted in any form or by any means,
electronic or mechanical, including photocopying,
recording, storage in an information retrieval system,
or otherwise, without the written permission of
the publisher.

MILLS & BOON and
MILLS & BOON with the Rose Device
are registered trademarks of the publisher.

First published in Great Britain 2003
Large Print edition 2003
Harlequin Mills & Boon Limited,
Eton House, 18-24 Paradise Road,
Richmond, Surrey TW9 1SR

© Leigh Michaels 2003

ISBN 0 263 17920 6

Set in Times Roman 16¼ on 17½ pt.
16-0703-49901

Printed and bound in Great Britain
by Antony Rowe Ltd, Chippenham, Wiltshire

X·1967

CHAPTER ONE

THE longer Mr. Pettigrew talked, Kimberley realized, the more his voice sounded like the drone of a tired housefly. Add the fact that his office was small, dry and overheated, and it was no wonder she was feeling a little dazed, as if she were about to slide into a trance. If it hadn't been for the man sitting next to her, across the desk from the interminable Pettigrew...

Perhaps it was a good thing after all, she thought, that Mr. Pettigrew had scheduled a joint interview to announce his decision about who would get the contract to print his company's annual report to the stockholders. At least sitting next to Tanner Calhoun was helping to keep her alert.

Without turning her head, Kim tried to get a sideways glance at Tanner. But his chair was too close to her own for her to see much except his hand, which was lying in apparently perfect relaxation on the knee of his gray trousers. He had long, strong-looking fingers, the nails short and neatly shaped.

5

And I'll bet, Kim thought, *that his palms aren't even sweaty, which means I won't have the satisfaction of seeing him ruin the perfect crease in his trousers when I snatch this contract out from under his nose.*

She could live without that triumph, of course. Still, it would be nice for once to absolutely know that Tanner Calhoun wasn't quite as cool as he seemed.

Mr. Pettigrew was still droning, but suddenly the nasal sound of him saying Kim's name yanked her out of her half-hypnotized state.

Here it comes, she thought. *Gotcha, Tanner Calhoun.*

"So thank you, Ms. Burnham," Mr. Pettigrew said, "for tendering your bid. It was a close decision, and I hope you'll bid again on our future work." He stood up. "Mr. Calhoun, I'll send over the copy and the final specifications this afternoon so you can get started. As you know, this project is quite a time-sensitive one and I'm anxious to have it underway."

He didn't sound anxious. He sounded as if he were reading the dictionary.

Kim's ears were ringing. She simply couldn't have heard right, she told herself. Maybe she'd dozed off after all and was having a nightmare right in Mr. Pettigrew's office.

But he was standing up, reaching across the desk to shake Tanner Calhoun's hand. It was over, and Kim knew when she was beaten. She stumbled to her feet and dutifully mouthed her thanks to Mr. Pettigrew for considering her proposal.

Somehow, before she could reach the door, Tanner was there to open it for her. "Ever the gentleman," she said under her breath. "Except where money's concerned."

His left eyebrow quirked. "Surely you wouldn't want me to patronize you by fixing my bids in order to let you win, Kim."

"Of course I wouldn't!"

"Then what are you complaining about? Are you in such desperate straits that losing Pettigrew's job is going to force Printers Ink into the red?"

"Even if I was, I wouldn't tell you my troubles," Kim said irritably. "Why must you always have that subtle twist in your voice when you say the name of my business, anyway?"

"Because it's such a cute little thing."

"The name, or the business?"

Tanner appeared to consider. "Both, actually."

She wanted to storm away from him, but he dropped into step beside her to walk down the hallway. "I should have had that contract," she said finally. "I underbid you."

He looked mildly interested. "It would be nice to know why you're so certain of that. I wonder whether you're only guessing or you have a source inside my office."

Her conscience wouldn't let Kim throw suspicion on his innocent employees. "Nobody told me," she admitted. "But my bid has to have been lower than yours."

"Perhaps mine was better in other ways."

A young man came out of a cubicle and hurried down the hallway after them. "Ms. Burnham," he called. "Ms. Burnham!"

Kim wanted to pretend she hadn't heard him—not because she wanted to ignore the young man, but because she didn't think what he had to say was any of Tanner Calhoun's business.

But Tanner paused politely. "It appears that Pettigrew Junior would like a moment of your time."

"I'm sure you won't want to wait," Kim told him sweetly. "After all, the specs will be arriving at your office any minute, and I'm sure you'll want to get right on such an important job."

"Oh, I don't need to be in any hurry. That's the real advantage of my new presses—they're not only fast but they're efficient."

So the rumors she'd heard about Calhoun and Company's new equipment were true. And Tanner hadn't installed just a single new press, it seemed, but a whole array of them. *Maybe he underbid me after all,* Kim thought. *He's going to need every job he can get—no matter how thin the profit margin—to pay for that.*

Tanner was still talking. "And since I hope to be working with the Pettigrews for a good long time, I should be on the same familiar terms with the next generation as you are." He looked over her shoulder as the young man approached and murmured, "On the other hand, perhaps not *quite* as familiar as you are."

Kim glared at him and turned to face Jasper Pettigrew. He was very young, very thin, and very earnest, and his blue eyes behind his thick glasses were almost worshipful. "Ms. Burnham, I wanted you to know I tried awfully hard to convince my father. About your bid, you know.''

''Thank you, Jasper,'' Kim said. ''That was kind of you.''

''I just wanted you to know. I wish I could have done more, but he…'' He shot a look over his shoulder. ''I have to get back into my office.''

''Of course.'' Kim felt like patting him on the head.

He ducked back into the cubicle. Kim didn't look up at the man standing beside her.

''Ah,'' Tanner said, and pushed open the front door for her. ''Now I see why you were so certain you should have gotten the contract. Shame on you, Kim. Using your deadly feminine wiles to convince young Jasper Pettigrew to manipulate his father.''

Kim raised her chin. ''I suppose next you're going to tell me which part of that scenario amuses you more—the idea of me having feminine wiles, or of Jasper Pettigrew having influence over his father.''

''Oh, I wouldn't dream of saying anything of the sort. I am, as you yourself pointed out, a gentleman. Can I buy you a cup of coffee?''

He might as well have come straight out and said it, Kim thought, because the implication was so very clear. If he couldn't tell her what he thought because it wouldn't be chivalrous to do so, then what he thought certainly wasn't flattering. She was wondering how on earth a man could be so impossibly rude while sounding absolutely polite, and the question he'd asked almost slipped by her unnoticed.

When it finally registered, she stopped dead in the doorway. "Coffee? What for?" She knew she sounded astonished, and she didn't care. "Because you feel sorry for me, losing that bid?"

"I wasn't thinking of cappuccino as a consolation prize. I'd like to talk to you. You know, just chat about what's going on, how's business—"

"You think I'd tell you?"

"Then it's not going so well."

"I didn't say that," Kim snapped. "Why? Are you going to offer to throw a job my way? What's wrong with it that you want to get rid of it?"

"Kim, you are incredibly suspicious. I just want to talk to you."

She looked up at him thoughtfully, eyes narrowed. "Careful, Tanner. You don't want to sound desperate. I wouldn't have thought a man in your position would have any trouble finding a woman who *wanted* to have coffee with him, but when you beg like that it really makes me wonder. No, I can't have coffee with you. I'm afraid I have something far more important to do this evening."

"Let me guess." He didn't stop beside the row of parking spaces reserved for guests, where she'd noted that his Mercedes was parked, but kept pace with her across the lot toward the train platform on the corner. "Washing your hair? Doing your nails? No, you wouldn't be so predictable. I've got it— you have to rake the gravel in your hamster's cage."

Kim bit her lip hard.

"I'll be damned." Tanner sounded astonished. "You almost smiled. You tried to hide it, but you actually almost—"

"I have a hot date with my roommates," Kim said firmly. "Once a month we sort out the long-distance bill and figure out who owes what. There's my train, if you'll excuse me."

She was already on the platform when he called, "The phone bill? I thought you'd be more original than that, Kim. I'm disappointed in you."

"Good!" she called back. "I like it when you're disappointed!"

The pizza was long gone, but the aroma of pepperoni was still hanging in the air by the time the phone bill was sorted out. Kim leaned against the arm of the couch and studied the printed list of calls. "This is actually sort of pathetic," she said finally.

Marissa, who was sitting on the floor beside the trunk which served as a coffee table, scraped up the last bit of cheese from the pizza carton and popped it into her mouth. "What's pathetic?"

At the other end of the couch, Brenna held out a hand and studied her nails. "She means the fact that three incredibly attractive, talented and fascinating women don't have anyone better to call than our assorted relatives. There's a fallacy in that reasoning, of course."

Marissa nodded. "I wouldn't exactly say we're *incredibly* attractive."

"Speak for yourself, darling," Brenna murmured.

Kim grinned. "Oh, I see. You mean there's one of us in each category. You're obviously claiming to be the incredibly attractive one, Brenna, so that leaves Marissa and me to fight over which one of us is talented and which one is fascinating." She tossed the bill onto the trunk.

It actually wasn't all that far from true, Kim thought. Beside Brenna's cover-girl good looks, her own dark-brown hair and green eyes were merely ordinary, and Marissa faded into the shadows altogether. At the moment, however, Kim didn't feel either talented or fascinating, and Marissa seemed to agree.

"Personally I'd settle for being either one," Marissa said. "Maybe we should take a poll before we decide. Of course, I have no idea who we'd ask—the only guys I run into these days are more worried about acne and cracking voices than the opposite sex. Which reminds me, I have essays to grade before school tomorrow." She stood up.

Brenna stretched as gracefully as a cat. "And that wasn't the fallacy I meant, anyway. Men are supposed to be calling us, not the other way around—so of course the calls don't show up on our bill.''

''Maybe you could tell the men that,'' Marissa said glumly. ''They don't seem to have gotten the message. Anyone for chocolate?''

''Not me,'' Brenna said. ''I was up a pound this morning, so it's steamed broccoli for me for a few days. I shouldn't even have smelled that pizza. You know, Marissa, if you'd ever go somewhere besides school—''

Marissa had returned from the kitchen with a bag of peanut clusters. ''You mean the singles bars? No, thanks. They're tiresome—it's sickening to hear the same old lines over and over. That's the biggest problem with modern life, you know. There is no good place to meet men. Singles bars are boring, personal ads make a woman look desperate—''

''Aren't you?'' Brenna said slyly.

''No, I'm *not* desperate. I just want someone to date.''

''Personally I'd prefer a *lot* of someones,'' Brenna mused.

Marissa was on a roll. ''The Internet's dangerous because there's no telling if the guy you're talking to is really who he says he is.''

"In fact," Kim murmured, "there's no way to know if he's really a guy."

"Exactly my point. Dating someone at work is a sure way to mess up your life—"

"There's always the old gimmick of joining the church choir," Kim said.

"The last time I tried that," Marissa said darkly, "the handsome tenor went home with the baritone in the back row."

Brenna clapped her hands sharply, and the other two abruptly stopped talking. "As a matter of fact," she said, "you're wrong, Marissa. It isn't meeting men that's the problem. We all know plenty of them."

"And how many of the men you know do you want to date?" Skepticism dripped from Marissa's voice.

Brenna shrugged and admitted, "None. Maybe I know them all too well."

"So there's no romantic air of mystery about them?" Kim sat up straight. "That's it. Take Tanner Calhoun, for instance—"

"I'd take him at the drop of a hat," Brenna murmured. "And I've never even met him, only heard you ranting and raving."

"That's my point. He drives me nuts, but maybe he's just right for you. How will you ever know, though, if you don't meet him?"

Brenna closed her eyes. "I'm warning you, Kim. Depress me any more and I'll tackle Marissa for the chocolate."

"You're right, Bren, we all know plenty of men," Kim said. She was feeling triumphant. "We just need to swap them around."

"And how do you propose to do that?" Marissa bit into another peanut cluster. "Trade address books?"

"There has to be a way." Kim frowned. Down deep inside her a bubble of excitement was forming, the same bubble that always told her when she'd struck on a really winning combination to offer a client. If she could just pull the pieces together.... "We'll have a party," she said slowly. "If we each invite, say, three women..."

Marissa frowned. "Wait a minute. Women? I thought the whole point was—"

"There will be twelve of us altogether. And if each of those twelve women invites two men—"

Brenna opened one eyelid. "You mean men she doesn't want to date?"

"Exactly," Kim said. "Men she knows but doesn't feel romantic about. By the time the party's over, each woman will have met more than twenty new guys—guys who we'd never meet in our ordinary lives."

"There's got to be a catch," Marissa said.

"Well," Kim mused, "we'd have to be sure that every woman understood the rules. She has to vouch that the men she brings are single, sane, self-supporting…"

"Straight," Marissa added.

"Not on parole," Brenna tossed in.

"We can work out the details," Kim said. "After all, every woman there will be in the same boat. They'll all understand."

"The men might object to a party where they outnumber the women two to one."

"It's just a party." Marissa put down the bag of chocolate. "At least, the guys don't need to know it's anything but a regular party."

"The Bachelor Bazaar," Kim said dreamily. "It would be just like a smorgasbord."

Brenna sat up straight. "Throw me that phone bill."

Kim reached for it. "Why?"

"Because I'm going to use the back of it to make a list of the women we're inviting. *And* the men. There's a new guy at one of the photo agencies I've been working with…. Who are you bringing, Marissa? The new principal at your school?''

''Maybe. I'll have to think.''

''And you, Kim? Who's your second invitation going to?''

Kim was startled. ''What do you mean, my second?''

''Because the first one's already decided.'' Brenna began to write, then looked up, eyebrows arched. ''You'll be bringing Tanner Calhoun. Won't you?''

Usually, when Kim got off the elevated train at the stop nearest her office, she tried not to look at the building across the street from Printers Ink. Though it was far newer than her own, the gleaming glass and steel structure had been there almost as long as she could remember. And for almost as long as she could remember, it had been a thorn in her side, too.

It was bad enough, she thought, that she had to go head-to-head against Tanner Calhoun in nearly every job she bid for these days. But it was more annoying yet for the two firms to be located not only in the same industrial park but on the same street. Why Tanner's father hadn't chosen to relocate, when he'd built the new headquarters....

"Because he found it far more satisfactory to know that my dad would have to look at that shiny glass and steel every day," she muttered. And she had to admit that Ben Burnham had reacted just as Charles Calhoun had expected he would. Ben had never been resigned to the idea that his old partner had done so well after their breakup, while his own business—though it was successful enough to support a family— was hardly a barn burner in the profits department. Watching her father through the years was why Kim had learned not to look at the building across the street.

But today she didn't have much choice, because she was going to have to call Tanner Calhoun and ask him to a party.

How was it possible that something which had seemed to be such a good idea could end up being so troublesome? The Bachelor Bazaar was a natural. People networked about jobs and mentors and higher education and career changes every day, so why not apply the same techniques to the most intimate of interests—

finding Mr. Right? It was a practical modern solution for a practical modern problem.

If only she hadn't mentioned Tanner Calhoun last night.

Not that he didn't meet the criteria the three of them had tossed out. *Single*...check. *Sane*...well, underbidding her on the Pettigrew deal probably wasn't the most brilliant move he'd ever made. Kim had sliced her price to the bone, so Tanner couldn't possibly make any money if he actually was doing the job for less. But that was hardly the same kind of mental problem as hearing voices which weren't really there.

Self-supporting...not even a warning blip on the radar. Lots of men in Tanner Calhoun's position dressed well, drove a Mercedes, and worked in a shiny steel building, but did it all on borrowed money. Tanner wasn't one of them. His shiny steel building had been paid for long ago, and if his wardrobe and his Mercedes weren't, it was only because he hadn't yet gotten around to writing the checks. His credit rating was like platinum; Kim knew it because a client had told her just a couple of months ago, while explaining why he'd decided to go with Calhoun and Company instead of Printers Ink.

Straight.... She had no doubt about that, either. Though they didn't generally move in the same social circles, there was an occasional Chamber of Commerce event that they both attended—and whatever else Tanner might be wearing, there was always a blonde clinging so closely to his arm that she appeared to be part of his sleeve.

Not always the same blonde, of course. And, now that she stopped to think about it, Kim had to admit it wasn't *always* a blonde. Last Christmas they'd both turned up at the Christmas party hosted by the development firm which operated the industrial park, and the woman who'd been drooling on him then had been a redhead.

If there was one thing Tanner wasn't, it was desperate for feminine companionship. Which was what made that invitation to coffee yesterday very interesting indeed. Kim almost wished she'd taken him up on it—if only because then she wouldn't have been home to look at the phone bill last night, so she wouldn't have made the offhand comment which had ultimately led to the whole idea of the Bachelor Bazaar.

Which brought her right back to where she'd started, except that now her head hurt.

The moment she opened the front door of Printers Ink, Kim knew things weren't going to improve anytime soon. A tall man was standing with his back to the door, his hands braced on the reception desk, looming like a vulture. The receptionist was saying, "I'm sorry, sir, but our CEO hasn't come in yet. If you have an appointment—"

"*If?*" The man snorted. "How dare you suggest I don't know what I'm talking about? My time is valuable, and if your CEO can't remember appointments then I'll take my business elsewhere."

Kim was racking her brain. Surely she couldn't have forgotten something as important as a meeting with a client—and if so, why didn't she recognize the client? Even from the back there should have been something familiar about the man.

Marge, the receptionist, caught a glimpse of Kim and looked relieved. "Here's our CEO now, sir," she said.

Kim braced herself as the man started to turn.

"It's about time you showed up," he bellowed. "I've only stayed this long for the satisfaction of telling you that I'll never—" He stopped dead. "You're not the CEO."

"I beg your pardon?"

"The CEO's a man."

Talk about a dated attitude. Kim took a firm grip on her composure. "My name is one that's sometimes given to a male," she said. "Perhaps that's what confused you."

The man shook his head. "Never heard of a woman named Tanner."

A mix of irritation and relief swept through Kim. "That explains it," she said. "You have the wrong building. You want that one—over there." She pointed out the front door.

He looked confused. "But this is the printing company. Isn't it?"

"Yes—and the building across the street is another printing company. You might want to hurry, though. Mr. Calhoun is a busy man— and he's almost as impatient regarding his appointments as you are."

She watched till he had crossed the street and vanished into the glass and steel building, and only then let herself sag with relief. "Now that's one client I'm glad to lose," she said under her breath. "One thing about it, Marge, the day has to get better from here."

"I wouldn't bet on it," the receptionist said dryly. "Your stepmother's waiting for you in your office."

Kim rubbed her temples. "You wouldn't happen to have an aspirin, would you?"

She swallowed the tablet with a gulp of coffee and, still carrying the half-full cup, pushed open the door to her small office. Sitting at the desk with papers strewn over the blotter was a tall, white-haired woman wearing a scarlet suit that screamed its designer's name. Kim took a closer look at the papers and felt her blood pressure begin to rise.

"Good morning, Letha." Kim kept her voice steady, but it took effort. "I don't recall asking you to stop by to take a look at the profit-and-loss statement."

Letha Burnham didn't take her eyes off the papers. "I have every right to inspect the books whenever I choose. I still have a stake in this operation."

In a manner of speaking.

Kim didn't answer. Finally Letha pushed the pages aside and looked up. "Not doing very well, are you, Kimberley?"

"We had a difficult quarter," Kim conceded.

The office door opened behind her. What was the matter with Marge, Kim wondered. She certainly knew how taxing a session with Letha could be—she'd started working for Ben Burnham back when Kim was a toddler, before her mother had died and Ben remarried. So why was she interrupting?

The receptionist muttered, "Phone call, Kim."

Kim smothered a sigh, but she didn't question Marge's judgment about how important the matter was. "Excuse me, Letha."

"It can wait until I'm finished," Letha said firmly.

Kim pulled the telephone across the desk. "Kim Burnham."

A lazy masculine voice murmured, "Good morning."

Speak of the devil, Kim thought. In the three years since she'd taken over at Printers Ink, she'd never talked to Tanner on the phone—but on the one morning she was going to have to brace herself to call him, he'd beaten her to the punch.

He went on, his voice sounding like warm honey. "I understand I have you to thank for my first appointment of the morning being late and in a peculiar state of mind.''

With Letha to think about, Kim had almost forgotten the troublesome would-be client. ''I didn't upset him on purpose,'' she said defensively. ''As soon as he made himself clear, I sent him across the street.''

Letha's gaze sharpened. ''Are you talking to—''

She didn't say the name. Kim didn't remember her ever saying it, as a matter of fact.

Kim turned her back to the desk. Curiosity was getting the better of her. ''Was he still furious when he got over there?''

''As a matter of fact, he seemed quite deflated. He even apologized for being late and said you told him I was a stickler for appointments.''

''Not exactly,'' Kim demurred. ''I was just trying to hurry him on his way.''

''And out of *your* way.''

''That, too. Look, Tanner, as long as I've got you on the phone...'' She swallowed hard. *This is really going to send Letha through the roof.* ''I wondered if I could buy you a cup of coffee.''

The silence was so long and complete that she wondered if he was still on the line.

"Sometime," she added feebly. "Whenever it would be convenient."

"Careful, Kim. You don't want to sound desperate. When you beg like that—"

She interrupted, wincing at the irony of him quoting her own words back at her. "I just want to talk to you. That's all."

"Come over about one," Tanner said. "I'll give you lunch."

"That's not what I had in—"

But he had hung up before she could finish the sentence. Slowly, Kim put the telephone down. Lunch. Well, at least she'd have plenty of time to ask her question. *Gee, Tanner, wouldn't you like to come to this party I'm arranging?*

Talk about sounding desperate, Kim thought.

Letha's eyes were little more than slits. "Your father would have been ashamed of you."

Kim sighed. "I've got a busy day, Letha, so let's cut to the chase. What do you want this time?"

*   *   *

The street seemed very wide. Kim waited for a couple of trucks to pass before she stepped off the curb, but finally there was no more excuse for delaying.

Because of its sheer size, she had expected Tanner's building to be almost cavernous. Instead the atrium lobby she stepped into felt more like the sunroom of a nice suburban home, large enough to be airy, but filled with plants and comfortable furniture. High in an enormous ficus tree, she caught a flash of yellow just an instant before a canary began to sing. Near the small desk was a trickling fountain.

Birdsong and water flowing. How odd, she thought, that she couldn't hear the rhythmic thump or the heavy roar that were the characteristic sounds of a running press. It was a sound so ever-present at Printers Ink that—like her own heartbeat—she had almost stopped hearing it.

The young man behind the desk stood up to greet her. "Welcome, Ms. Burnham," he said before Kim could give her name. "Mr. Calhoun asked me to show you to the conference room. May I take your coat?"

He showed her through an archway behind a potted palm and down a hallway, throwing open a door. Kim stepped in, and with a little bow of his head, he closed the door behind her and was gone.

She gave a soundless whistle and walked across the room. The far wall was a single huge sheet of glass and she stood beside it, feeling breathless as she looked down a full story at Tanner Calhoun's new presses. She had known the building was large before she'd ever entered; now she realized that in fact fully two-thirds of it lay underground. Far below where she stood, workers moved from post to post, watching and adjusting. A forklift slid silently up and bore away a pallet stacked with finished work.

The door opened almost silently, and she turned away from the window to face Tanner.

"It's one of my favorite views," he said softly. "Don't let me keep you from enjoying it."

"It's impressive," she conceded.

Tanner stepped aside as a caterer's assistant rolled a cart into the room and began to arrange two place settings at one end of the conference table.

Kim was startled.

"I invited you here," he said, "because we can talk more comfortably in private."

Malarkey, she wanted to say. *You invited me because you expected that the home court advantage would intimidate me.*

But if she challenged him, then she'd have to admit it had worked—and that was the last thing she wanted to do.

She looked out over the press room again. It was so well-insulated, so soundproofed, that only now could she begin to sense the vibrations from the enormous machines. Or was it her own heartbeat she was feeling as her nervousness grew?

Tanner came to stand beside her. "Now," he said, "tell me—what has inspired you to suddenly ask me for a date?"

CHAPTER TWO

TANNER had intended it as nothing more than a careless comment, something to break the ice. But he was startled by the response to his off-hand words. Kim's eyes, the clearest jade-green he'd ever seen, went wide and dark with something that looked like shock.

How had that simple question managed to strike such a nerve?

"D-date?" she asked.

"I was just trying to lighten the atmosphere," he said dryly. "You know. Teasing."

"Oh. Well, you asked me to coffee yesterday, and I couldn't go. I just thought I should find out what you wanted."

In a pig's eye, Tanner told himself.

The waiter finished laying the table and set two covered plates in place. Then he moved the cart till it was still within reach but not blocking the table, and he faded away.

"You must do this a lot," Kim said, "if you don't even have to give directions to the caterer."

Tanner held her chair and took the one at the head of the table. Lifting the covers off the plates, he set them aside on the cart. "Not a caterer, exactly. We contract with a food service company. They post menus in advance, and our employees sign up—or go out for lunch if they don't like the food choices."

Kim raised her gaze from the colorful mix of rice, vegetables and chicken on her plate. "You feed your employees like this every day?"

"They pay a fee for the meal, but the company subsidizes the cost. It ends up being less expensive for us in the long run. If employees go out for lunch, it takes longer for them to get back to the job and be productive afterward than if they just walk the length of the building to the dining room."

Kim looked thoughtful. With the tines of her fork, she gently moved a snow pea from atop her rice.

"I took a guess on the menu, of course," Tanner murmured. "The other choice today was country-fried steak, if you'd rather have that."

"Oh, no, this is fine. I just...." Her voice trailed off.

"You're wondering why I'm going to the trouble."

"Well...yes."

"It's been just about twenty-five years since your father and mine decided that they couldn't be business partners anymore. It seems to me it's time to bury the hatchet."

Kim looked wary. She stopped even pretending to pay attention to her food and put her fork down. "But that doesn't make any sense, either. My father died almost two years ago, and yours has been gone—"

"Much longer than that."

"So why right now? Why not last year, or next year?"

"Because last year I didn't think of it, and next year seems too long to wait when we could benefit in the meantime."

"Benefit? Like how?"

She didn't sound wary anymore, Tanner thought, she sounded absolutely dubious. It didn't come as any surprise to him, though, that she was boring in on the details. In the last two years, she'd showed herself to be a painstaking competitor.

Instead of answering, he changed the subject. "Do you still have that Ripley press?"

"You mean the one that caused the partnership to break up because my father bought it and yours didn't approve?"

So that had been Ben Burnham's explanation of the split. "Family folklore is such an interesting thing, I think," Tanner murmured. "There's always such a difference in perspective in how events are explained."

Kim drew herself up straight. "I suppose that means your father accused mine of stealing company funds to bet on the ponies."

"Not quite. Anyway, whatever happened doesn't matter anymore. Do you still have the press?"

"Yes. It's not for sale."

"I don't want to buy it. Butter for your dinner roll?"

Kim shook her head. "No, thanks. If you're not trying to buy it, then why do you even care whether I still have it? It's not an antique, it doesn't have sentimental value and it's certainly no piece of art."

"I want to pass on some work to you." *That did it,* Tanner thought as he watched her eyes turn the turbulent emerald of a storm-tossed sea. She'd gone from wary all the way through dubious and now she was positively dripping mistrust.

"That's big of you." Her almost-polite tone didn't match up with her narrowed eyes. "Throwing crumbs my way."

"You're every bit as touchy as your father was, aren't you, Kim?" He added deliberately, "And suspicious to boot."

A dull red flush rose in her cheeks as though she was embarrassed, but she said stubbornly, "It takes some nerve for you to say that to me."

"Not really. I'm sure the breakup of that partnership was caused by fault on both sides. They always are. But the point is, what happened back then doesn't matter anymore. The sooner we get past that baggage, the sooner we can do ourselves both a favor." He broke his dinner roll in half and buttered it meticulously. "My new presses are fast and efficient. Sometimes they're too fast and efficient."

"Such a problem," Kim murmured.

"It can be. Now and then one of my customers wants a smaller job. One of them, last Christmas, wanted to send out his holiday greetings in the form of a minimagazine."

"Cute."

"Not from where I'm sitting. My presses run so fast that we usually ruin three thousand copies of whatever we're printing just to get the ink adjusted right. On a print run of half a million, that kind of spoilage is nothing. But in this case—"

"How many did the customer actually want?"

"Five hundred," Tanner said dryly. "It was not a profitable job."

Kim nodded. "Because you couldn't possibly charge him what the work was worth, no matter what it cost you to do it."

"Exactly. It's a matter of customer service, and that always has a cost."

"I've had a few of those myself. There also seems to be a law that the smaller the job is, the bigger the nuisance factor."

"Amazing, isn't it? The most finicky people are the ones who are spending the least money. But the important thing isn't that I didn't make anything on that job, it's that doing it tied up my production line and kept me from moving along on other work."

"The big and really lucrative projects, you mean."

"There's nothing wrong with making a profit, Kim. The point is, I can't make money on a small job like that, and it's a nuisance. But your Ripley press could have handled it easily, and it wouldn't have blown your regular work schedule out of the water."

"So next time," she said, "send the customer across the street to Printers Ink. I'll take care of him."

He had to give her credit, because she'd said it with a perfectly straight face. "You know better than to think I'd do that."

Kim smiled as she admitted, "It was worth a try—but obviously you aren't going to tell your clients to take their small work somewhere else, because their big jobs might follow."

"That's just about the size of it. I was figuring out how much money we lost on that funky little Christmas-card magazine, and it occurred to me that I could subcontract that work to you. I'd be happier, because I wouldn't be tying up my presses with jobs that cost me money. My customers would be happier—they don't care how or where the work is done, only that they get results. You'd be happier, because with your smaller, older equipment, you can turn a profit on the little jobs where I can't."

"I wouldn't say I'm exactly *happy,*" Kim said.

What did she expect? That he'd offer to renew the partnership? "Fine—you don't have to throw your hat in the air with joy. But you must admit it's a fair offer. Better than fair—it's a good offer."

"And there's another benefit for you—isn't there, Tanner? If you can toss me enough of those little jobs, I'll be too busy to look out for the big ones. And if I'm not bidding against you, you can price your work however you like."

Tanner's father had sometimes referred to his one-time partner as Bulldog Ben, though Tanner had never quite known why. Now he understood—because, he thought, there was a distinct family resemblance between Ben Burnham and his daughter. Once she took an idea between her teeth...

"Frankly, Kim," he said coolly, "now that my new presses are up and running, you can't compete with me on the big jobs."

"Oh, really? I guess we'll just see about that." She pushed her chair back.

"You may as well finish your lunch before you go," Tanner said. "Because that covers

why I invited you to coffee—but you still have
to explain why *you* invited *me.*''

Kim sank slowly back into her chair. In her
irritation over Tanner's proposition, she'd entirely forgotten the Bachelor Bazaar.

*Well, Brenna is just going to have to do with-
out meeting Tanner Calhoun,* she thought. *Because if I never see him again myself after this,
it'll be too soon.*

Though, when she stopped to think about
it... Wouldn't there be a kind of compensation
in inviting him to be her guest, when her real
intention was to palm him off on someone else?
He'd probably be flattered that she had thought
to ask him—and she could nurse the secret satisfaction that he had no idea what was really
going on... Yes, that was it.

Before she could talk herself out of it, Kim
said airily, ''Oh, that. I was just going to ask
you to a party.''

Obviously a party hadn't even been on the
list of things he'd considered, for Tanner's eyebrows rose as high as they could possibly go.
He said softly, ''No wonder you reacted so
strangely when I asked if you wanted a date.
Because—''

"Of course it's not a—" She stopped short, but it was too late.

"Then if it's not a date, what do you call it?"

"Just a party," Kim said lamely.

"What kind of party?"

"Now who's being suspicious?" She'd been wrong, Kim realized. His eyebrows *could* go higher. She tried to regain the ground she'd lost. "Oh, for heaven's sake! It's only a get-together my roommates and I are having this weekend at our apartment. That's all."

"Just some people you thought I might like to meet?"

Kim sensed a trap yawning, but she couldn't quite put her finger on where it lay. "Yes," she said warily.

"Generally, the guest list for a party includes people who have something in common," Tanner mused. "You know—they all share an interest in politics, or hang-gliding, or wife-swapping. What's the common factor in this case?"

Actually, wife-swapping comes pretty close, Kim thought. "Only that they know Brenna, Marissa, or me." As explanations went, that should be safe enough—and it even had the advantage of verging on the truth. "Brenna's an aspiring actress who does a bit of modeling as well. Marissa teaches English to thirteen-year-olds at a private boys' school."

"And you run a small business."

Not all that small, Kim wanted to say. But the comment was almost funny—because the size and relative profitability of Printers Ink was probably the one thing on earth that Tanner and her stepmother would actually agree on.

"Do you have these parties often?"

Never before. And—I swear—never again. What was I thinking of? "We entertain from time to time."

"It must be an interesting mix of people," Tanner mused. "Considering the different lives the three of you lead."

"Some are more interesting than others. But I thought you might enjoy the party."

"It's sweet of you to be concerned about my social life, Kim."

"Saturday evening, seven o'clock." She gave him the address and had the satisfaction of seeing a flicker of surprise in his eyes.

"Those lakefront towers are some of the most expensive real estate in Chicago," he said.

"That's right. Sorry to ruin your image of me and Printers Ink, Tanner, but I'm doing just fine without you throwing work to me."

"Of course, there are the roommates," he said. "Splitting the rent three ways must make it almost affordable. Think about my offer, Kim. I could keep you busy most of the time."

"Oh, I'll think about it. Just don't hold your breath waiting for me to grab the opportunity."

"I won't," Tanner assured her. "Because holding my breath would imply there was some doubt about whether you'll agree in the end." He took a plate from the bottom shelf of the caterer's cart and lifted the cover off. "Would you care for dessert? I see it's double-fudge brownies today."

The rents in the high-rise might be sizable—Tanner had been absolutely correct about that—but the apartments themselves weren't, and so the three of them had spent much of the day rearranging the furniture in an attempt to make enough space for thirty-six people to mill around, talk, nibble on snacks and get to know each other.

"They'll never fit," Marissa announced. "I told you we should have reserved one of the common rooms downstairs."

"There's a reason they're called common rooms," Brenna said. "It's because they have no personality. But if the Bachelor Bazaar is going to work, it has to be an intimate sort of party, not just another cocktail affair where nobody listens to each other."

"Just as long as nobody decides to have an even more intimate party in my bedroom," Marissa muttered. "Remember? We've never met most of these people."

"Relax, would you?" Brenna said impatiently. "Getting acquainted is the entire point!"

Kim finished stuffing another tray of mushroom caps and set them aside, ready to go under the broiler. "Not every last person we've invited is going to show up," she said. "They never do, for any kind of party."

Brenna eyed her narrowly. "Are we talking about anyone in particular? Because now that I think about it, you haven't said much of anything about Tanner Calhoun all week. Is he coming?"

I haven't the foggiest. "I'm sure if he doesn't show up there will be a good reason." *Some really good reason...like he never intended to.*

"He'd better," Brenna threatened. "Because it would really look bad if the hostesses' own guests don't make an appearance."

"Who will know? We're not exactly going to go round the room for show-and-tell." Kim washed the rest of the spinach stuffing mix off her hands and let her voice rise to a girlish treble. "*'Hi, I'm Sally, and I brought my ex-husband to share—really, girls, he's all right, I just got tired of him falling asleep right after making love, so I divorced him. And I also brought the guy who's remodeling my closets, because he keeps making passes at me and I'm tired of it so I want to shift him on to someone else.'* That kind of introduction would sort of give the whole thing away, don't you think?"

Marissa snorted. "It would be priceless to watch the ex-husband's face."

"Well, I'm going to be keeping track," Brenna announced. "Every woman's supposed to bring something for the snack table, right? I'll just usher each one aside as she arrives, relieve her of her food contribution and make her write down the essential information about her two men. Name, age, place of employment—"

"So if they don't show up you can go after them anyway," Marissa murmured.

"So we know which of our friends we can rely on to deliver the goods," Brenna said firmly. "Because we may want to do this again."

Heaven forbid, Kim thought, and with the last of the food preparation done, she went to change her clothes.

The doorbell started ringing while she was getting dressed, and by the time she returned, the living room was already filling up. Half a dozen people were gathered around the high counter that separated the small kitchen from the living room, already sampling snacks. Marissa was adjusting the volume of the background music. Brenna was at the refrigerator, digging for a diet cola.

She'd have better luck finding it, Kim thought, if she would look at the shelf instead of fluttering her eyelashes at the man who was waiting for the drink.

Another man was standing alone by the half-wall which set the minuscule foyer apart from the living room. He had his back to the crowd and he was seemingly entranced by the empty aquarium which had been built into the wall. "I wonder why they don't have any fish in this thing," he said ingenuously as Kim walked by.

"Mostly because we've never got around to buying any," Kim said. "The aquarium was already here when we moved in because the previous residents installed it. If we take it out we'd have to destroy the wall. On the other hand, since none of us are particularly interested in fish, we just use it as a night-light."

He blinked at her. "You live here? I feel like I'm crashing your party, because I wasn't exactly invited."

Not invited? Now that's interesting. "You're certainly welcome, regardless. Um—did you come with someone?"

"Yeah." He scowled across the room. "My sister. She insisted that I bring her."

That was certainly one way to get an unsuspecting bachelor to the bazaar, Kim thought.

"She told me she doesn't feel safe in downtown Chicago at night," the man went on. "Which is a bunch of bull, if you ask me. Betsy has never said anything like that before, but suddenly tonight she panics at the idea of coming into the city by herself."

Kim searched her memory. Betsy—wasn't that a fellow teacher of Marissa's? She could see the man's point; if the neighborhood around St. James prep school didn't faze his sister, Lake Shore Drive shouldn't, either. "Well, whatever the reason, I'm glad she brought you along. What's your name?"

"Mine? I'm Dan. So now that we're here, she leaves me standing here twiddling my thumbs while she's over talking to that guy at the snack bar."

"Sorry," Kim said cheerfully. "But we don't allow thumb-twiddling at our parties. There's Marissa over at the stereo—do you know her?"

Dan followed her nod. "No, don't think so."

"Then I'll introduce you." The doorbell rang. Kim glanced around hopefully, but of the three of them, she was closest to the entrance. "Just hang on a second till I get this." She pulled the front door open and said, "Wel—" Then her voice died in midword.

Tanner looked down at her, and then past her to the young man standing next to the aquarium. "You appear to be surprised. You did say seven o'clock—didn't you?"

Caught wrong-footed, Kim spoke before she thought. "I thought... You never said you were coming."

"I never said I *wasn't* coming," he countered. "Which I certainly would have done, if I had been unable to accept your flattering invitation. Because after all I am—"

"I know, I know," Kim muttered. "You're a gentleman. Give it a rest already. Come in and make yourself at home while I introduce Dan around."

She ushered the young man across the room, introduced everybody and left Dan to help Marissa choose the music. Then she headed across the living room to the snack counter.

Tanner followed. "The young man seemed very disappointed when you abandoned him like that," he observed.

"Marissa will take good care of him." Kim noted that the first batch of stuffed mushroom caps had already vanished, except for a single small, limp, and lonely one which seemed to be stuck to the serving tray. She picked up the tray and started to work her way through the crowd so she could put another pan under the broiler.

"I think he'd much rather have had you," Tanner observed. "He's looking at you just about the same way the big guy in the corner is eyeing that last mushroom on your pan.''

Kim glanced around, saw the big guy in question, and held out the tray. Smiling a bit sheepishly, the man scraped it loose. ''These are really good,'' he said. ''Did you make them?''

''Guilty,'' Kim admitted.

Brenna had finally located the diet cola on the bottom shelf of the refrigerator. As Kim came around the counter into the kitchen, she handed it over. The guest, still seeming a bit bemused by Brenna's smile, tried to open the can while he was still looking at her.

Kim, seeing an accident in the making, took a step backward to avoid the almost inevitable spray of cola and collided with something solid, warm and definitely male. A pair of arms closed around her, and Tanner set her back on her feet. ''Good thing I was handy,'' he murmured in her ear.

''Why are you following me? Go enjoy the party.''

''I *am* enjoying the party. After all, you're the one who invited me. It would be rude of me to go hang out with someone else. Besides, mushrooms are one of my favorites, too.''

Brenna swung around from the still-open refrigerator. "You must be Tanner," she purred. "I'd have recognized you anywhere from Kim's description."

"That's a bit frightening," Tanner said.

Brenna laughed. "Come sit in a comfortable corner with me and I'll tell you everything she said." Even in the dimmer-than-normal light, her perfectly manicured red nails contrasted sharply with the navy sleeve of Tanner's sports coat.

Brenna's fingernails looked like talons, Kim thought. It was no more than Tanner deserved, of course.

"Yes, do," Kim said pleasantly. "I'll bring you a mushroom as soon as they're done."

"Don't hurry," Brenna murmured. Without a glance back at the hapless diet-cola drinker, she drew Tanner off into the living room.

Kim gave a sigh of relief. She closed the refrigerator door that Brenna had left standing open and put another pan of mushrooms under the broiler, hovering close until they were done.

Just as she was lifting the hot pan out of the oven, the big guy appeared again. "Is everything else you cook as good as these?" he asked, eyeing the still-sizzling mushrooms.

"Hardly. I can make three things, and this recipe requires two of them."

He looked disappointed. "What's the other one?"

"Spaghetti—but only if the sauce comes out of a jar." She spooned all but one of the appetizers onto a serving plate and set it on the counter.

"But if you're not a cook, why are you the only one in the kitchen?"

"Because somebody has to be, and my roommates are even more inept with a paring knife than I am. Excuse me, I have to take one of these into the living room." She scooped the last mushroom onto a napkin and went in search of Tanner and Brenna.

It took a while to find them, because they weren't together. Brenna was dancing with a tall blond man in the middle of the living room, and Tanner was in the corner talking earnestly to Marissa.

What an irony, Kim thought. *Brenna was dying to meet him, but it turns out she's not his type—Marissa is.* Though how that fit together with the gorgeous dolls Tanner was usually escorting was beyond her. Not that she intended to waste any time trying to figure it out. She'd warn Marissa, of course, but beyond that it was none of her business.

Suddenly she realized that Tanner was no longer focused on Marissa but was watching Kim intently as she crossed the room. Kim could almost feel the weight of his gaze, and she noted that Marissa was looking up at him with a tiny frown between her brows.

Kim held out the napkin. ''Just as I promised, one mushroom. So take the covetous expression off your face before someone concludes it was me you were looking at instead of a mere appetizer. We wouldn't want anyone to get the wrong idea.''

''You only brought me one?'' Tanner bit into the mushroom, and still-hot juices spurted over his fingers. ''On the other hand, maybe I should be grateful. This isn't an appetizer, it's a weapon.''

Kim smiled at Marissa. ''Don't blame me because you're not patient enough to let it cool.'' She headed back for the kitchen.

The big guy was still there, only now he was looking through the cupboards. He'd found a couple of half-filled bags of chips somewhere and adopted the clips which had been holding them closed; now the clips fastened a towel to his belt and formed a makeshift apron. "I hope you don't mind," he said briskly.

"Mind you moving into the kitchen?" Kim said faintly. "Of course not. Why should I mind?"

He gave her a sidelong look. "People do sometimes. I'm Robert, by the way." He pulled a bag of soft tortillas from the cabinet and looked thoughtfully from it to the array of cans and bottles he'd already excavated. "I think we can do something with this."

"Not me," Kim said quickly. "I'll just watch."

He smiled a little.

Across the counter, a skinny man in glasses poked at a mushroom with a toothpick. "What's wrong with ordinary food?" he said plaintively. "Why do women have to ruin everything by adding green stuff?" He scooped up a handful of chips and wandered off.

Robert reached for a knife and tested the blade. He shook his head. "I wish I had my steel," he said. "I'll bet every knife in this kitchen needs to be sharpened."

"Both of them," Kim agreed. She watched as the blade of his knife flashed, chopping something she didn't recognize until it was so fine it was almost a paste.

One of Brenna's friends leaned across the snack counter. "Is that you, Robert? Honestly—can't you stay away from food for two minutes?"

It was obviously a rhetorical question, for she moved away before Robert could answer.

"Is this a hobby or a profession?" Kim asked.

He started to smear the paste onto a tortilla shell. "I'm a chef at the Captain's Table."

"It isn't much of a party for you, if you're working just as usual."

He shrugged and started to roll up the tortilla. "I like cooking much better than talking to strangers."

"You don't seem to have any trouble talking to me."

He didn't look at her. "You don't feel like a stranger. Here, try this." He sliced the end off the rolled tortilla and offered it to Kim.

Brenna sidled up beside her. "Have you met everybody yet, Kim?"

Kim shook her head. "I suppose you have."

"Almost. Except for the artist I hear is hiding out in the kitchen." She flashed a smile at Robert.

He turned a little pink.

Brenna murmured, "Your Tanner is quite the charmer."

"Not mine," Kim pointed out. "I'm surprised you aren't still talking to him."

"And miss out on the other twenty-three? My dear girl... Besides, you don't impress a man like that by hanging on him."

"I see," Kim said. "Or by telling him how much you've looked forward to meeting him, I suppose." She popped the tidbit Robert had offered into her mouth and started to chew.

"I was merely indicating interest," Brenna said firmly. "One does, after all, have to break the ice or one would never get anywhere."

Kim rolled her eyes and caught a glimpse of Tanner coming up behind Brenna. She tried to swallow so she could warn her roommate, but she hadn't realized till then that Robert's idea of an appetizer was man-sized. All she could do was wave a hand at Brenna, moan, and keep on chewing.

"But I would never allow Tanner to monopolize me all evening," Brenna went on. "It would make me look desperate."

"On the contrary," Tanner said pleasantly. "Kim says I'm the one who looks desperate." He leaned back against the counter, propping himself with both elbows, and looked out across the crowd. "You know, there's something awfully odd about this party."

Brenna's jaw had dropped and she appeared unable to speak. Robert was concentrating on another tortilla. Kim swallowed and said, "I imagine you'd like one of us to ask why you think something is wrong. All right, I'm game. Why?"

"I didn't say wrong, I said odd. The proportions are off. Way off—there are twice as many men as women. Quite an unusual group for a party."

"We have lots of male friends," Kim said, trying to sound careless.

Tanner's eyes narrowed. "How about introducing me to all of them? If they're all your friends...."

"Well, mine and Brenna's and Marissa's." *Time to bluff, Burnham.* "But all right. Let's start with Robert here. He's a chef at—"

Tanner interrupted. "And Robert's last name is…?"

"Yaskowitz," Robert said.

Kim tried not to look relieved. "Thanks, Robert. You know how much trouble I have pronouncing that right."

Tanner turned back to the crowd. "How about the skinny guy with glasses?"

"The one who hates green food?" Kim asked brightly. "That's Jake…uh…Jones. Isn't it, Brenna? Or have I got him mixed up with the computer guy?"

Brenna was still looking dumbstruck. "What?"

"I'm dying to meet him," Tanner said gently. His hand closed on Kim's elbow and he drew her out of the kitchen and across the living room.

"All right," she admitted. "I don't know his name after all. He came with one of Marissa's friends, I think. What's the big deal, Tanner?"

He didn't answer until they'd reached the corner where the empty aquarium glowed. "Oh, nothing much. I'm just the curious sort." He looked down at her, smiled and said very deliberately, "For one thing, I'd like to know how many of these guys know they're being surveyed for a stud book.''

Kim gulped.

''I'm betting it's none of them,'' Tanner mused. ''So the other thing I'd like to know is what they'll say when they find out.''

CHAPTER THREE

WAS it only the glow of the lights inside the empty aquarium, Tanner wondered, or had Kim's face actually turned slightly green?

"Stud book?" she said faintly. "I haven't any idea what you're talking about."

"A stud book is—"

"I *know* what it is. I just don't have any idea why you think anyone would—"

"Would be compiling one that lists Chicago bachelors? I can think of several reasons, myself."

"Tanner, that's downright insulting!"

He had to give her credit. It hadn't taken much time at all for Kim to recover enough from the shock to try to turn the tables on him. Not that he was about to let her get away with it, of course.

"It's insulting for the bachelors, yes," Tanner said smoothly. "But I admit I may have been too blunt in calling it a stud book, so let me rephrase the comment. You've assembled a group of men here tonight—without telling them why—so that a much smaller number of women can look them over, check them out, and sum them up, for purposes which shall for the present be left to the imagination. Is that better?"

"Not much." Her tone was tart. "The fact is that the only purpose of this evening—if you insist that a party have a purpose at all—is to have fun."

"Oh, no. You're not going to get me to buy that explanation, because every woman here has that kid-in-a-candy-store look about her."

"I haven't the vaguest idea what you're talking about."

"You're not dense, Kim, so stop pretending to be. You know exactly what I mean. Every woman in this room is looking around as if she's got only a dollar to spend, but she has to decide between a few hundred different kinds of chocolate."

Kim shrugged. "An interesting comparison, I suppose, but—"

"And an accurate one. Look over there, for instance. Your roommate is talking to one man, but she's already eyeing the next one on her hit list."

"You mean Brenna?" Kim didn't even bother to glance in the direction he'd pointed. "Obviously you don't know her very well, because she always does that."

"As a matter of fact, I was talking about the other one."

Kim's eyes widened. "Marissa?"

"Is that her name? Sorry, I'd forgotten. You may as well tell me, Kim. What is this—some kind of flea market where every woman brings her discards and you all trade?"

That had clearly been a hit, he realized—he could tell by the way Kim's shoulders slumped that he'd struck pretty close to the bull's-eye. But the reaction lasted only a moment before she pulled herself up straight. "Not discards, exactly." She sounded just a bit defensive.

"Well, that's some relief for me, since you can hardly discard what you never possessed in the first place."

Acute dislike flared in her eyes, but Kim went straight on as though she hadn't heard the interruption. "We agreed to bring men we're not personally interested in, not necessarily ones we'd dated."

"The stud swap," he murmured. "So now you can all paw through the merchandise and take home whatever you like."

"Would you stop it? It's not as boorish as you're making it sound!"

"Then what are you calling it—a white-elephant exchange? I'm dead sure I don't like being thought of as a useless decoration, either."

"Stop twisting everything I say, Tanner!"

"So tell me what you've named it, and I'll stop speculating. And don't tell me it doesn't have a name, because—knowing you—I'm sure it does."

She bit her lip.

"Come on, Kim," he said. "Talk—or I'll tell every man in the place that he's part of a mating dance."

"The Bachelor Bazaar," she said. Her voice was so low he had to bend closer to hear. In the crowded room, it was the first time he'd been able to smell her perfume—a soft, musky scent that seemed to pull at his tie, tugging his head down. He restrained himself before he could bury his nose against the soft spot under her ear where she must have dabbed the scent.

Get a grip, Calhoun, he told himself.

"And every man here should be flattered to be included," she added defiantly.

The instant the words were out, however, she looked as if she regretted letting the comment escape—which made Tanner even more anxious to hear how she was going to explain it away. "Really? Why?"

She hesitated and looked over his shoulder. "Because there were some requirements in order to make the cut."

"Must be listed in Dun and Bradstreet," he speculated. "Have a solid gold credit reference. Be able to prove future earning power—"

"Do you really think that all a woman is interested in is money?"

"Of course not. I'm sure you considered genetic potential, too. After all, we need to watch out for the future of the race."

"For heaven's sake, this is only a way to meet people—it's not some cold-blooded experiment in breeding!"

"Oh, that's a relief. So what were the criteria?"

She said mulishly, "I'm not telling you."

"Okay, I'll start asking all the guys what they've got in common." He swung around to face the crowd.

Kim's hand closed on his sleeve. "Don't! I mean, you can't—you said you wouldn't say anything to anybody if I told you the name we gave it."

"No," Tanner countered. "I said I *would* talk if you *didn't* tell me. Now I want to know what distinguishes a man who got into the Bachelor Bazaar from one who couldn't make the grade. Or is simply having testosterone and a heartbeat enough?"

Kim pressed her lips firmly together.

"You know, there are guys who would take that expression as a challenge," Tanner murmured, "and try to kiss you out of your sullen mood."

"Don't even think about it."

"I didn't say I was one of them." He relented. "Oh, all right...why should I ruin your fun? As long as I know what's going on, it's nothing to me whether every other man here gets caught in the nets."

Relief dawned in her eyes.

It was pure mischief that made him go on. "It's actually a pretty good idea," he mused. "Far more manageable, for instance, than having a garage sale. I don't know about all these other guys, but I'd object to sitting on a table in somebody's carport with a price scrawled on my forehead.''

Despite what he'd said about playing along, after that last remark, Kim couldn't let him wander around the party by himself for fear of what he might say and to whom. Considering Tanner's twisted sense of humor, she was afraid he might find it hilarious to go around to every man at the party and ask how he'd feel about being a garage-sale item.

But, she concluded hopefully, if she stuck to him like glue for the rest of the evening, perhaps that too-sensitive and completely annoying perceptivity of his wouldn't turn out to be a calamity after all. Tanner might know one or two of the other men who had been invited—though she doubted many of them moved in the same social climate, because no one else at the party had shown anywhere near the level of suavity that was Tanner's natural aura. So it was a pretty safe bet that once the party was over, he was unlikely to ever run into any of these guys again. As long as she could keep him from talking to them in the next couple of hours...

With that in mind, she set out with grim determination to keep him entirely to herself.

It was soon clear to Kim that Tanner knew exactly what she was doing. He didn't comment, but there was an unmistakable twinkle in his eyes. After the first few minutes he very deliberately tucked her hand into his elbow and kept it there, and within half an hour he'd politely told one of Marissa's friends that he couldn't talk to her because Kim would strenuously object if he divided his attention between her and another woman. The woman gave Kim the dirtiest look she'd ever received.

"You know," Tanner said earnestly as the woman turned her back and walked away, "I'm sure if you put your mind to it you could think of a better way to keep me occupied for the rest of the evening."

By doing what? Taking you back to my bedroom?

Kim snorted. "Not in this lifetime."

Tanner seemed nothing more than mildly curious as he asked, "Then you don't want to go out for a midnight drink somewhere that would be quieter than this?"

Kim choked. "A drink? You were asking me out for a drink?"

"A drink," he said calmly. "Why? What were you thinking about, my dear? Something more...intimate, perhaps?"

"Nothing," Kim managed to say. "It's a little late to be going out, that's all. The party will be winding down soon."

"That doesn't mean we have to wind down with it. There's a coffee spot a few blocks away. If we'd stop there for a shot of caffeine, we could stay up all night." Then, as if he knew she had no intention of answering, he nodded to the skinny guy with glasses. "I understand you're interested in computers," he said. "But I didn't catch your name."

The young man looked blank. "Of course I'm interested in computers. Isn't everybody?"

Tanner winked at Kim. "Do you have a business card? I might find a use for your services."

The young man pulled a card from his breast pocket, and with a laugh Kim snatched it out of his hand and crumpled it into her pocket. "I'm sure I asked you not to get all wrapped up in business tonight," she told Tanner. "Naughty boy." She tugged hard on his arm, and the skinny young man, looking puzzled, turned back to the snack bar and another handful of chips.

As the party began to break up, Tanner murmured something about not wanting to wear out his welcome. Kim was momentarily comforted by the idea of finally getting rid of him, but the relief soon faded. If he went out with a group of other guests, and talked to them on the long ride down in the elevator…anything might happen.

"No," she said firmly. "Please stay a little longer."

She kept him beside her until the last guests were gone and just Brenna and Marissa were left. Only then, when the final group had had plenty of time to disperse from the building, did she walk Tanner to the door and practically push him out.

With him finally gone and the interminable evening over, she turned with a sigh of relief to meet twin looks of incredulity from her roommates.

"What in heaven's name got into you?" Brenna demanded. "Hanging on him like that! You're the one who set up the rules, Kim. You shouldn't have invited Tanner to the party in the first place if you wanted to keep him for yourself."

Kim felt a bubble of hysteria rising inside her. "Want him? Want him?" she said shrilly. "Of course I don't want him! *Hanging on him like that* is the only thing that saved us from calamity. He was ready to tell every man here...." Words failed her. She shook her head and fell into the nearest chair. "Just let me tell you this—both of you. I don't ever want to hear the words *Bachelor Bazaar* again. So if you've got that—" she closed her eyes "—then everything's all right."

They all slept late on Sunday morning. By the time Kim struggled out of bed, trying to fight off the headache that had accompanied her persistent nightmares, Marissa was sitting in the living room with a cup of black coffee and a look of stunned disbelief as she contemplated the mess left from the night before.

"Let me get some caffeine, too," Kim said, "before we start clearing up the wreck."

"Maybe we should just move to another apartment," Marissa muttered. "No—another city. It would be a lot easier than cleaning up."

"You go drag Brenna out of the sack, and I'll start picking up the litter."

"Oh, no," Marissa said. "I'm not taking my life in my hands by waking her up before noon. If you want her up, you do it."

Kim jumped a foot as the telephone rang at her elbow. Who would be calling at this hour on a Sunday morning? Probably nobody who had been at the party—they would know better. Nobody who wanted to talk to Brenna—because her friends were the same sort of night owl that she was. Nobody from Marissa's school—their weekends were every bit as precious to them as to Marissa.

Which left only a few possibilities. And of them, the most likely was Letha Burnham, who often checked in on Sunday mornings. As if, Kim thought, she kept hoping to find her stepdaughter nursing a blinding hangover. She forced herself to smile—wearing a smile colored the tone of one's voice, a speech coach had once told her—and picked up the phone.

But it wasn't Letha's clipped syllables she heard on the other end of the line, but a low masculine voice, full of lazy humor. "Good morning," Tanner said. "Did you have a pleasant night?"

"Oh, much better than the evening was. And you?"

"I didn't get much sleep, I'm afraid. I was far too busy thinking of the possibilities."

"Possibilities for what? Blackmail?" Kim shifted the phone to the other hand. "If that's why you're calling me this morning, Tanner, let me tell you I have no intention of—"

"My dear, nobody said I was calling you."

Kim stopped dead. "What does that mean? Of course you're calling me. You dialed my number—"

"But I didn't ask for you," he said, sounding patient. "You're simply the one who answered the phone."

"So who is it you want to talk to?"

"Your roommate will do. Marissa—was that her name? Such a charming young woman. I'd like to get to know her better. After all, that was what your party was all about—getting acquainted with new people—and when I had a chance to think it over, I realized what a very good idea the Bachelor Bazaar was. Congratulations, Kim. I mean, it was your idea, wasn't it?"

Kim took a long sip of her coffee and tried to gather herself.

"Kim?" He sounded so earnest that if she could have reached through the phone line, she'd have slugged him—and she suspected he knew it. ''I do hope I haven't hurt your feelings by asking for Marissa. After you paid such close attention to me last night, too—''

She tried to smother her growl and handed over the phone to Marissa. ''For you,'' she said. ''But watch out, because he's up to something.''

She picked up the nearest handful of paper plates and plastic cups and carried them into the kitchen. It would have been rude to listen in— and worse yet, Kim admitted, it would have been useless to try. The apartment was small, but Marissa's end of the conversation consisted mostly of monosyllables.

So Kim pushed the debris into the wastebasket on top of last night's garbage and gloomily checked the contents of the refrigerator to see if there was something suitable for breakfast.

Finally Marissa got off the phone and came straight into the kitchen, sounding so full of energy that Kim wanted to go pull a pillow over her own head.

''We have to get this mess cleared up right away,'' Marissa said.

''Why?''

"Because Tanner is coming over in about an hour."

Kim shrugged. "He saw the destruction last night. He's not going to scream and run from it now." *More's the pity.*

"Still, it looks so much worse in daylight, and I wouldn't want him to think we're all slobs."

"Particularly you," Kim said dryly.

"Well, naturally." Marissa started running dishwater. "He's such a delightful man, don't you think? Oh, I forgot—of course you don't think he's delightful or you wouldn't have invited him to the Ba—" She broke off midword and eyed Kim cautiously.

"You must admit I have a little more experience with him than you do."

"Perhaps too much," Marissa said calmly. "It's given you a prejudice. I just hope you can be pleasant to him when he comes."

"Oh, I'll be pleasant even if it kills him. I mean, even if it kills me."

Marissa leveled a look at her. "On the other hand," she said firmly, "it might be better if you had to go out for the morning."

"And miss seeing Brenna's reaction when Tanner comes courting you? Not on your life, Riss."

"Courting is such an old-fashioned word," Marissa objected.

"Well, it seems Tanner is an old-fashioned sort of guy. I wouldn't have thought it, but when he got all bent out of shape at the idea of women taking the initiative to meet new men... You two must have had quite a conversation last night, in order to develop this mutual admiration society. When did that happen?"

A tiny frown etched itself between Marissa's eyebrows. "And your reason for asking is...?"

"Pure curiosity."

"Good. Because I wouldn't want to worry that you were being jealous, or anything silly like that."

Kim started to laugh. "Me? Jealous? You are absurd, Marissa."

From the doorway, Brenna yawned. "Was that the phone that woke me up?"

"It wasn't for you. But in case you're planning to keep score, Bren—Marissa has the first request for a date."

"Doesn't bother me a bit," Brenna said with another enormous yawn. "I wouldn't accept a date with a guy who had so little sense as to call me up at this hour on a Sunday morning anyway.''

"Maybe he'll take you out for brunch, Marissa," Kim speculated.

"You mean the date's this morning, too?" Brenna looked stunned. "I'd better do my makeup if we're having company."

"I'm sure he'll have eyes only for Marissa." Feeling much better, Kim pulled out a dish towel and began drying the dishes Marissa was washing. "I'll finish this. Go get dressed, Riss. You don't want to greet him in your pajamas."

"Not on the first date, anyway," Brenna murmured. "Save that treat for later."

Brenna's normal morning routine took at least an hour, and Marissa seemed to be primping for the occasion. Kim, on the other hand, didn't much care what she looked like, so she threw on jeans and a loose-knit cotton sweater and got the vacuum cleaner out. She was just finishing the living room when the doorbell rang.

Marissa was nowhere in sight. Kim sighed and pulled the door open. "Don't get any ideas just because I'm the one who happens to be answering the..." Too late, she realized that it wasn't Tanner who was standing on the welcome mat. "Oh. Hi, Robert."

Somehow, the chef looked even bigger in the hallway than he had in the kitchen last night.

"I was on my way to work when I thought about those dull knives of yours," he began. "And since I brought my steel with me this morning—"

He took a small bundle from under his arm. It was a lumpy little package that looked as if he'd grabbed handfuls of wrenches and hammers and wrapped them up in a dish towel. Kim hoped he never had to stop at the bank on his way to the restaurant, because a sensitive teller might well assume he intended to rob the place. He certainly looked equipped to do so. "I thought you'd already be at work. Doesn't the Captain's Table do lunch on Sundays?"

"Yes, but I mostly work the dinner crowd these days," Robert said. "I'm just going in a little early today to place my food order for the week. Anyway, I decided to take a chance on finding someone at home. It'll just take a minute to sharpen your knives and then you'll be all set."

"Sure." Kim stepped back from the door. "If you're certain that it's no trouble. It's very nice of you to think of us."

Robert led the way to the kitchen and set the bundle on the counter. "Everybody's afraid of a really sharp knife, but actually there's nothing more dangerous than a dull one. Instead of cutting cleanly, they slip—and that's how people get hurt." He unfolded the bundle.

The wrapping wasn't a dish towel after all, Kim realized, but an enormous apron. Inside the careful folds lay an assortment of deadly looking knives and peelers, plus a few spatulas and a couple of wooden spoons.

"I like to use my own tools." Robert started opening drawers so he could look for knives.

"I gathered that," Kim said faintly.

The doorbell rang again. There was still no movement from the bedrooms, so Kim went to answer it once more. Tanner appeared perfectly at ease, standing on the welcome mat with what appeared to be a brown paper grocery bag cradled in one arm.

"If you're planning to impress us with your wizardry in the kitchen," Kim told him, "you've got competition already in residence."

"I never set foot in a kitchen if I can help it."

"So what's in the bag, if it's not lunch?"

Tanner peered into the bag as if he'd forgotten what it contained. "I suppose you *could* call it lunch, but only if your taste buds aren't terribly delicate."

Robert reappeared with a knife in one hand and a sheet of paper in the other. "Look," he said with an air of satisfaction. He held up the paper and sliced it with the knife, creating a row of deep parallel cuts. "That should do it. This isn't a bad knife, really. If you treat it with respect, it will last for a lifetime, but if you use it carelessly—"

Brenna interrupted from the hallway. "Honestly, I turn my back for a minute and all sorts of exciting people show up," she murmured. Her gaze darted back and forth between Tanner and Kim and then settled on the chef. "It's Robert, isn't it? Marissa's still getting dressed but she'll be along in a moment—I hope you don't mind waiting for her. Tanner, we'll forgive you this time for catching us unprepared, but you know you really should call before you stop by."

"Oh, but he did," Kim murmured.

Tanner said gently, "Thank you, Kim, but I can handle this. I'm the one Marissa's expecting. I believe Robert's here to visit Kim."

Brenna concealed her shock almost instantly. If Kim hadn't known her so well, she might even have missed the momentary bewilderment that flashed over Brenna's face.

"Well, actually," Robert began.

"Robert came by just to sharpen our knives," Kim said quickly.

"I see," Brenna said dismissively. "That's very thoughtful of you. Having a sharp knife will make opening my mail much easier."

Robert winced in pain. "No," he protested. "You should never use a good kitchen knife to cut paper."

Brenna shrugged. "Why on earth not? You just did." She moved closer to Tanner. "I should have known *you* were too much of a gentleman to simply drop in."

Robert opened his mouth and shut it again without uttering a syllable. He retreated to the kitchen. Kim, rolling her eyes, followed, to find Robert working with swift efficiency to pack up his tools once more.

"I'm sorry about that," Kim said. "I'm afraid it wasn't very polite of Brenna to imply that you..." *And I'm not making it any better,* she thought, *by repeating the insult!*

"It wasn't what she said about being a gentleman," Robert muttered. "But to open her mail with a good knife—"

"Oh, that. I thought I'd warned you that both Brenna and Marissa are even more helpless in the kitchen than I am."

From the living room came a happy squeal, and a moment later Marissa appeared in the kitchen.

"You sound delighted about something," Kim said.

"Wait till you see what Tanner brought. I need some water to put them in." She looked around as if puzzled.

"Flowers?" Kim asked. But that bag he'd been carrying hadn't suggested flowers to her.

"You'll find the water in the sink," Robert said under his breath. "*H* for hot, *C* for cold."

Marissa laughed merrily. "No, silly, I was looking for something to put water in, to carry it into the living room. Something big, because I need to fill the aquarium before Tanner can put in the fish."

You could call it lunch, but only if your taste buds aren't terribly delicate, Tanner had said.

"Fish?" Kim said weakly. "Why on earth did he bring fish?"

Marissa looked a little sheepish. "I suppose because I told him last night that I've always wanted to start up the aquarium, but I'd just never gotten around to actually doing it."

Kim stared at her. "Riss, I never knew you wanted fish."

"Well, I'd like to have a pet of some sort. Dogs aren't practical in a high-rise, Brenna's allergic to cats...."

"That's hard to believe," Robert said under his breath.

Kim could almost hear what he was thinking. *Because she is one.* She bit her lip to keep from smiling.

Robert tied up his bundle. "I'll get out of your way. You've obviously got a lot to do."

"It was very nice of you," Kim said, following him across the living room. She was feeling a little desperate. Poor Robert—he'd only been trying to do them a favor, but he'd ended up feeling like an intruder—unwelcome and unnecessary. She had to do something so he wouldn't leave on this disillusioned note. "Don't rush off, Robert."

Brenna sniffed. She had sat down on the end of the couch, swinging a sandaled foot as she flipped the pages in the newest issue of her glamour magazine. ''I want everybody to know I'm having nothing to do with a bunch of slimy fish.''

Robert paused to look at the row of plastic bags standing on the coffee table, each containing a fish in a bubble of water. ''Ordinary goldfish?''

Tanner took a pitcher from Marissa and poured water into the aquarium. ''The clerk at the pet store suggested starting off small and easy, with fish that are fairly adaptable. Goldfish can handle various conditions, but some of the tropicals require precise temperatures and daily attention.''

''Which they're not likely to get around here,'' Robert said very quietly.

''On the other hand,'' Brenna said, ''if you'd all agree to make it a useful aquarium and fill it with lobsters, I'd be in favor.''

''It's not a big enough tank,'' Robert said.

''I didn't plan to keep them as pets, only to invite them for very brief visits. And I'll bet if you asked nicely, Kim, Robert would agree to give you cooking lessons.''

Trust Brenna, Kim thought. The woman could be totally rude or absolutely brilliant, sometimes in succeeding moments. What better way to soothe Robert's wounded feelings than by asking him to share his specialty?

"What a great idea," Kim said. "Then all your work in sharpening the knives wouldn't be in vain."

Robert looked interested. "Cooking lessons," he said, as if to himself. "I've never done that—I mean, other than training a new sous-chef, but that's a different kind of teaching."

"You could do it," Kim said. "And just think of the favor you'd be doing all of us." She ushered him out the door. At least, she noted with relief, he was smiling as he pushed the button to summon the elevator.

She closed the door and leaned against it with a sigh. *One down.*

Brenna had looked up from her magazine. "That was pathetic, Kim. You might just as well have begged the man to come again. Don't you know anything about handling the male of the species?"

Tanner stirred the water in the aquarium. "I don't notice you being overrun with admirers, Brenna."

Brenna slapped her magazine shut and strode off down the hall without a backward look.

Marissa had gone on another water run to the kitchen. Kim took a quick look around and lowered her voice. "Look, Tanner—I know you're annoyed with me, but don't take it out on my roommates, all right?"

"You mean you didn't like me putting Brenna in her place?"

"No, actually Brenna can take very good care of herself. It's Marissa I'm worried about. She's a sweetheart, and if you lead her on—"

Tanner held up a hand. "Scout's honor. I wouldn't dream of it."

But though Kim didn't think he would actually lie, she still didn't trust him not to hurt Marissa. Men could be so obtuse about how their actions affected others....

But it wasn't just that fact which was bothering her, Kim realized. Something was wrong here. She just couldn't put her finger on what it was.

CHAPTER FOUR

IF THE Ripley press wasn't the noisiest piece of equipment ever built, it was certainly high up on the list. Even with her protective earphones in place, Kim could hardly hear herself think as she stood beside it on Monday morning in the pressroom at Printers Ink, waiting to talk to the man who was running it.

The Ripley was neither the most efficient nor the most elegant of presses, but it was good at what it did, and as the machine worked it created an economy of movement which had a beauty all its own. The claws reached out to pull a sheet of paper off the stack, moved it swiftly over the press plate, and shifted out of the way, already reaching for the next sheet as the platen came down with a thump. As soon as the pressure was released, a second set of claws pulled the printed sheet off and dropped it on a finished pile, and another blank was put in its place. On and on, one copy every two seconds—and the press could work that way for weeks without stopping.

86

She pulled a finished copy from the stack to inspect. Today the Ripley was printing the monthly newspaper for a nearby antiques mall that preferred an old-fashioned look. By Kim's standards it was a midsize job, the kind of steady, solid work that kept Printers Ink running from month to month. Tanner would probably consider it too small to be anything but an annoyance.

Perhaps, Kim thought, she shouldn't have been quite so quick to turn down his offer of subcontract work. If she could count on another dozen jobs like this one every month, her financial position would be much more flexible.

But if that security meant being beholden to Tanner Calhoun...

Allowing herself to count on spillover work from Tanner to keep her business afloat would be foolish, because it could come to a halt at any time. Just because he wanted her assistance right now didn't mean the work would still be there in a few months. Conversely he could— if he chose—keep her so swamped with peanut-size jobs that she wouldn't have time to tackle anything bigger.

He was correct that she couldn't compete with him on the really big contracts. But there were plenty of middle-size ones that she could do, and whatever Tanner wanted to think, she could do some of them more efficiently and for less money than he could.

Take the catalog for Westway Cosmetics, for instance. She needed to finish up that proposal, making sure that she hadn't missed the slightest detail in figuring what it would cost her to print the company's seasonal catalog, and deliver the paperwork to the corporate offices before tomorrow's deadline. Then she'd just have to wait for the company's decision about who would get their business. Kim expected it to feel like a very long week.

It was, of course, an extremely long shot. But if the job came through...well, it would be the biggest contract she'd ever landed.

She had almost missed the chance to bid, because when she'd opened the mail a month ago and found the specs, she'd assumed that Westway wanted a catalog similar to what they'd been putting out for years now—a glossy full-color spread which was far more than Printers Ink could handle. As soon as she'd seen the logo and the heading inviting bids to print a catalog, Kim had started to drop the packet in the wastepaper basket, muttering about the waste of time, energy and resources in sending specs to every print shop in Chicago.

But something had stopped her, and when she looked again, she realized that this project was very different from Westway's usual. A new look, the company said it wanted—and as she studied the specifications, Kim's excitement had grown. This she could do. And it could be an enormous step up for Printers Ink.

Marge came from the front office into the pressroom with a clipboard full of checks and letters for Kim to sign. "I'm going to the post office," she called over the rhythmic thump of the Ripley press. "If you can sign these now, I'll mail them right away."

Kim stepped out of the pressroom into the much-quieter shipping department next door, pulled off her earphones and reached for the clipboard. Her lone shipping clerk must be taking a coffee break, so they had the room to themselves.

"As I was paying the bills this morning," Marge said, looking at the wall instead of at Kim, "I couldn't help seeing the size of that check you wrote to your stepmother last week."

Kim put on her reading glasses and flipped through the papers, glancing at each before adding her signature. "As long as there's enough money to pay the bills, Marge...." *Then it's really none of your business.*

Not that she'd ever actually say that to Marge, because the woman had been working for Printers Ink before Kim could cross a street by herself. Though Marge wasn't technically a partner, she had almost as big a stake in seeing the business succeed as Kim herself did.

"Barely enough." Marge's voice was clipped. "Did you forget about that pallet of paper you bought last week?"

Kim bit her lip. Much as she hated to admit it, she had forgotten—the salesman had caught her on her way out the door to get the results of the Pettigrew bid, and she'd fingered a sample, nodded, signed the form he offered and sent him inside to talk to Marge about the details.

"The trouble with buying things on rock-bottom close-out sales is that we have to pay on delivery," Marge pointed out. "Besides, it's the principle of the thing that chews at me, Kim. It's robbery—what Letha's doing to you."

"She has an interest in the business."

"Lots of interest, I'd say," Marge said dryly. "But only in the bottom line, not in the work that has to be done to earn it."

Kim signed the last check and handed the clipboard back. "Before he died, my father asked me to make sure Letha had what she needed."

"Humph. And I suppose she *needs* a Caribbean cruise? I saw the memo you wrote in the check register."

"Look at it this way, Marge—it's two whole weeks when she won't be bothering either one of us. We'll make it. We've got that big direct mail ad circular coming up for Tyler-Royale—"

"Has that copy come in yet? I haven't seen it."

"It isn't due for a while yet. Anyway, once that job is finished we'll be rolling in cash."

"Till the next time Letha thinks she needs something," Marge muttered. "I'm sorry, Kim."

"For what?" Kim asked lightly. "Speaking your mind?"

Marge shook her head. "For letting her loose in your office that day. But I was certain the profit-and-loss statement was at the back of the bottom drawer.''

"It was. Don't blame yourself, Marge. Letha can sniff those things out like a tracking dog.''

"Good comparison,'' Marge muttered. "She even looks like one, with that long nose always stuck out in front of her.''

Kim had to smile.

From the doorway, a voice filled with relief said, "Here they are,'' and Kim turned to see who was looking for her.

Behind the shipping clerk stood Tanner, trim in a blue-gray suit that she suspected would match his eyes almost exactly.

Now what does he want? Kim wondered. It must be something very important to get him to cross the street. "Sorry to drag you all the way back here to find me.''

"Oh, I enjoyed the tour.''

"Tour?'' Kim wasn't sure she liked the sound of that. Though Printers Ink didn't exactly have any trade secrets, she wasn't wild at the idea of Tanner wandering around her building taking a good look at everything. Fortunately, at the moment she didn't have any work in-house which the client considered confidential—so even if he'd gotten a glance at her current projects, no big damage would be done. If they'd already been printing the ad circular for the Tyler-Royale chain of department stores, it would have been a different story.

"I think we walked through most of the building looking for you," Tanner said. "I got to see the pressroom—"

"Bet that was a real thrill," Kim muttered.

"Of course it was. That's the first time I've laid eyes on the infamous Ripley—definitely a memorable moment. And your finishing department...all those folding machines, just standing idle."

"If you're implying that we don't stay busy—" Kim caught herself. Why go asking for trouble?

His eyes glinted. "And numbering machines... I haven't seen one of those in operation for years."

"Some of our clients still like their invoices numbered the old-fashioned way. I assume you had a purpose in coming, besides wanting a tour?"

"Of course." Tanner's gaze rested for a moment on Marge, then on the shipping clerk.

Kim sighed. "I assume that means you want to talk in private. Fine, let's go back to my office."

"I wouldn't want to take you away from your work. There must be a good reason why you're all the way back here, so I can just tag along until you're finished."

Bet you'd like listening in while I talked to my pressman about how long it'll take us to print the Westway catalog, Kim thought. "It's nothing I can't put off till later."

She had forgotten, until she was standing in the doorway of her office, that the half-completed Westway bid was spread out across her desk blotter. Of all the places to leave it.... But she'd only intended to be gone a minute— and she hadn't been expecting visitors.

Had he already been in her office?

It was too late to do anything about it now. Even if he hadn't already taken a look, she wouldn't put it past him to be able to read upside down—it was a skill common among people who worked around presses—so he could be looking at it right now. Was it only her imagination, or had the Westway bid been the first thing Tanner's eyes fell on?

Even if he hadn't seen everything already, if she scrambled to put it away now, he couldn't help but realize how important it was—and any detail he might have accidentally spotted would take on even more significance in his mind.

In any case, there was no point in fretting about it. She'd have to treat it as unimportant and hope he hadn't seen enough to make him curious.

She gestured him to a chair, then perched on the corner of her desk, propping one hand at the edge of the blotter so it blocked at least part of the paperwork. "If this matter is too private to talk about in front of my employees, it must be pretty confidential. Which means you probably want to talk about either top-secret business dealings or your date with Marissa."

Tanner set his briefcase down beside his chair. "Which do you think it is?"

"Well, since we don't have any top-secret business dealings, I'll opt for Marissa. Did you have fun?"

"Oh, absolutely. What did she say about it?"

Kim shrugged. "Not much, actually. She just went around for the rest of the day looking pleased with herself."

"Did she now," Tanner murmured.

"Well, don't get a big head over it, because Marissa is notoriously easy to please. As you should know for yourself—a few goldfish and she's ready to melt." Kim tipped her head back and looked at him closely. "Of course, you'll have a job topping the goldfish. What are you planning to bring her next time? A puppy?"

"Why not? A golden retriever, perhaps—just to keep the theme going."

"I was joking, Tanner."

"I wasn't. But it's comforting to know that if I run out of ideas I can just ask you."

"Don't bother," Kim said dryly, "because next time I'll just suggest roses."

"You disappoint me," Tanner said. "Flowers are entirely too easy. But I'll happily give you credit for thinking of the puppy."

"Thanks anyway. But—"

"Actually," he said abruptly, "your first guess was wrong. I did come to talk about top-secret business dealings. I know you said last week that you weren't interested in my excess jobs, but I thought I'd give you another chance. Now that you've had time to think about it...."

Kim opened her mouth to repeat that she didn't want to work for him. Instead she heard herself say, "I guess it won't hurt me to listen."

She was astonished. What was she thinking of?

"That's a step in the right direction," Tanner said approvingly.

But it *wouldn't* hurt her to listen, Kim told herself. It didn't mean she had to agree to take every single job he wanted to throw at her—or, indeed, any at all. Besides, she thought suddenly, if she kept the lines of communication open, she'd no doubt find out a tremendous amount about his client base. It could be nothing but advantageous to her to know more about his business. If she knew who his customers were, the kind of work they commissioned, the way he ran his company...

It wasn't exactly kosher business practice, she admitted. In fact, it almost sounded like spying. But so long as she used that knowledge only to improve her own services and not to try to steal his clients, there wasn't anything wrong with it, either.

Tanner reached for his briefcase, set it on the edge of her desk and snapped open the catches. Kim felt like sprawling across the desk blotter to hide as much as possible of the Westway paperwork—but if she did, he'd probably take it as an invitation to share more than information.

It was only a random thought—so it was beyond Kim to understand why her mind suddenly filled to overflowing with images of herself and Tanner atop her desk, of his briefcase crashing unheeded to the floor, of the Westway specs shoved into a ball to form a flimsy pillow, of her arms reaching up to welcome him and his mouth coming down hard on hers....

"What's the matter?" Tanner asked.

Kim had to clear her throat. "Nothing."

"Are you sure? You looked as if you had a sudden pain."

Only a fleeting cramp in the imagination. "I'm fine. What's the job?"

"A weekly newsletter for the employees at a company that builds stuff like conveyer belts."

"Oh, that sounds fascinating."

"You don't have to read it. The copy comes in camera-ready, and you just do the printing." He pulled a folded sheet from his briefcase. "Nothing fancy about paper or ink. Just a straight black-and-white job."

"How many? And how much money?"

"Nine thousand copies a week. What would you charge to do that, if the CEO walked in here and asked?"

Kim did the math in her head and told him.

"I'll give you three cents more than that— each. And I'll still make a little on the deal."

She whistled. "You aren't shy about telling people what your work is worth, are you?"

"You can't stay in business long if you're trying to cut too many corners, Kim. Give people too good a deal and they don't appreciate it. They think if you're always the least expensive you can't be the best."

It was good advice, but Kim wasn't about to admit it. "If that's my free lesson for the day toward my MBA," she said lightly, "thank you very much."

"I thought you already had your degree."

"Sort of." She reached for the newsletter.

Tanner held it out of reach. "Is it a deal?"

"Why can't I look at it before I decide whether I want the job?"

"Because I'm not telling you who the company is until we have an agreement."

Kim thought it over. "Every single week?"

"Except for the one between Christmas and New Year's Day. The plants are all closed then."

"I think I can handle the hiatus." She eyed the paper. "Sure. I'll do it."

"Good." He handed her the newsletter and took an envelope from his briefcase. "Here's the copy for the first issue. They need the finished product by Wednesday noon. Bring it across the street on Wednesday morning and there'll be a check waiting for you."

For payment on delivery, Kim thought, she'd wheel the cart across the street herself. "It's a deal." She unfolded the newsletter and looked thoughtfully at the name of the corporation. It was one of Chicago's largest and most cash-rich industries. No wonder Tanner hadn't wanted to volunteer the information that Universal Conveyer was one of his clients—it might tempt a competitor to go after their business.

Tanner said, "What do you mean, *sort of?*"

Kim had to run her mind back over the conversation before she remembered what he was talking about. "Oh—you mean my degree? I have a bachelor's in business, but I was just starting my master's program when my father got sick, so I can't write MBA after my name. Why? Does it make a difference on whether you hire me?''

''No.'' He frowned. ''But it was almost too easy to convince you. I can't help but wonder why you changed your mind, Kim.''

''What are you talking about? You offer me a job with acceptable conditions and good pay, and then you're suspicious because I take it?'' She was feeling just a little guilty, as a matter of fact. Not that she'd actually go after Universal Conveyer's printing business—even if it wasn't for the ethical considerations, she couldn't possibly handle it—but she had to admit that the thought had crossed her mind. *If I had big enough presses...*

''I thought perhaps I'd have to blackmail you before you agreed,'' Tanner said.

Kim's jaw dropped. ''With what?'' Had he seen her Westway bid after all? If he had—and he threatened to take advantage of the fact... What a fool she was to hesitate because of ethics, when it appeared that snooping was part of Tanner's standard business routine!

''You're the one who gave me the idea,'' he said calmly.

Me and my big mouth, Kim thought. Why had she had to mention blackmail yesterday, when he'd called to talk to Marissa? "And what are you planning to hold over my head?"

"Marissa gave me the list of everybody who was at the Bachelor Bazaar."

The comment was so unexpected that it took Kim a minute to switch tracks. "I didn't know there actually was a list," she admitted.

"Brenna seems to have made a point of it."

Of course, Kim thought. Brenna had said she was going to get every name and phone number.

"At any rate, now I can contact every single one of those guys. So I was going to tell you, if you didn't want to take on a few small jobs, that I'd just invite them all to another party—and tell them what the last one was all about."

When Kim got home that evening, Marissa was sitting cross-legged on the floor beside the coffee table, painting her fingernails hot pink.

"Waiting for the phone to ring?" Kim asked lightly.

"As a matter of fact, no."

"Well, that's smart, because now that Tanner's got what he wanted, he might never call again. Whatever made you give him that list, anyway?''

Marissa shrugged. ''He asked for it. What did he do to you this time, Kim?''

Kim told her about Tanner's threat to blackmail her by blowing the whistle on the Bachelor Bazaar.

Marissa laughed. ''He's got quite a sense of humor, doesn't he?''

''A sense of humor? Marissa, you're deluded. You're taking your life in your hands, dating that man—and you deserve whatever dance he leads you on.''

''I thought you said he wasn't likely to call again,'' Marissa pointed out. ''You can't have it both ways. Anyway, he'll be here in an hour or so, because he's taking me to the school carnival tonight.''

''School carnival?'' Kim said blankly. *''Tanner?''*

''What's the matter? Are you having trouble picturing him taking part in a cakewalk?''

''That's putting it mildly. How did you manage to get him to agree to that?''

''I told him I had to go because I'm supervising the library club's booth for part of the evening, and I mentioned I had an extra ticket.''

"He actually volunteered?"

"He said it sounded like fun," Marissa said primly.

Kim shook her head in disbelief. "I didn't realize you were such a seductress, Riss. Watching Tanner might be better entertainment than the rest of the carnival put together."

"I can still get you a ticket. Five bucks and you can follow him around from booth to booth all evening and be amused."

Kim shuddered at the thought. "No, thanks. I have a bid to finish up tonight. And I wouldn't want to be the fifth wheel on your date, anyway."

"Oh, speaking of dates, you've had two phone calls since I've been home. One man didn't leave his name, just said he'd be in touch later."

"A telemarketer, no doubt."

"But the other one...." Marissa capped her bottle of fingernail polish, waved her hands in the air, and very carefully extracted a slip of paper from under a magazine on the coffee table. "Remember Dan?"

Kim had to think about it. "Oh, yeah—the guy who came to the party with his sister."

"I told him you'd be home anytime after seven."

"See? I can't possibly go to the carnival," Kim murmured. "I have to sit here and wait for the phone to ring."

She changed her business clothes for jeans and a sweater, settled on the couch and took the Westway paperwork out of her portfolio. She'd hoped to have it finished before leaving the office, but Rick, her head pressman, had looked gloomy over a couple of her projections. Kim still thought she was right and Rick was being unnecessarily pessimistic, but she admitted that he had a point about the need to leave a little room for wriggling, just in case. On a job as big as this one, she couldn't afford any mistakes.

She was soon absorbed in making the final adjustments to her numbers, and she hardly noticed when Marissa went off to get dressed, or when Brenna came home, dropped her heavy model's bag in the exact center of the living room floor and sagged onto the couch.

"Obviously a rough day," Kim said absently.

Brenna nodded. "Having two art directors on the job does not split the work in half or make the result twice as good. And the one I invited to the Bachelor Bazaar seems to have gotten the wrong idea altogether—he followed me around most of the day suggesting activities he thought I'd like to join him in. As soon as I get my energy back, I think I'll order the most calorie-laden dish that anyone will deliver. Care to join me?''

''I thought you were still on steamed broccoli.''

''That would require actually dragging myself into the kitchen, because no respectable restaurant would put something like that on the takeout menu.'' Brenna put her head against the back of the couch and closed her eyes. She didn't even open them when the doorbell rang.

Kim, with a pretty good idea of who was outside, scrambled her papers back into her portfolio before she got up to answer it.

Tanner was dressed less formally than she'd ever before seen him, in jeans, an open-necked shirt, and a leather jacket. He glanced past her and spotted Brenna. ''Well, if it isn't two-thirds of the unholy trinity.''

Kim rolled her eyes at him. ''And what would Marissa think of you including her in that description?''

"As a matter of fact, she told me it was hilarious."

"Well, of course she would have said that. She didn't want to take a cab home from your brunch date. She's still getting dressed—so come on in and have a seat, if you can find one." Kim settled herself on the couch once more, but she didn't get her paperwork out.

Tanner paused beside the aquarium, where three fantail goldfish were swimming in lazy circles, and tapped a fingernail on the glass.

Kim, watching from the corner of her eye, saw that two of the fish had turned to look for the source of the noise, while the third paddled on, seemingly unaware of the interruption. "We need to change those bulbs," she mused. "The colored lights make their scales look brassy instead of brilliant."

The telephone rang, and without opening her eyes Brenna reached out and snagged it.

Tanner's eyebrows rose.

"She can do it without fumbling, even from a sound sleep," Kim murmured.

"It's for you," Brenna said, eyes still closed, and unerringly held the receiver out toward Kim.

It was two minutes past seven, she noted. Dan must have been watching the clock, waiting for the moment when Marissa had told him Kim would certainly be home. It was flattering, in a way, she thought, that he was so eager to talk to her. Still, she couldn't help but wish that he'd waited another half hour, till there were fewer people around.

She untangled the phone cord and carried it around the corner and into the kitchen. Unfortunately, since there was no door to close and only a counter stood between her and the living room, the idea of privacy was more illusion than reality.

Dan had barely gotten started—in fact, he was still thanking her for the party—when Marissa came into the kitchen, brushing past Kim. She got a bottle of water from the refrigerator and said briskly, "It's not too late to come to the carnival, Kim."

"Carnival?" Dan asked, obviously puzzled. "I didn't think it was the right season for carnivals."

"Well, this one isn't exactly Mardi Gras," Kim told him.

Marissa made a face at her. "If you don't want to be a fifth wheel, invite him to come too."

Kim cupped her hand over the mouthpiece. "Riss, I don't think—"

Marissa seized the phone. "Hi, is this Dan? How about double dating? Yes...you and Kim. She really wants to go, but... It's at St. James Prep. We talked about my school at the party, remember? That's where it is, in the gym. All right, we'll meet you there in half an hour."

She put the phone down and rubbed her hands together with satisfaction.

Kim eyed her with caution and finally said, *"Kim really wants to go?* You know, Marissa, I'm not altogether sure I like the new assertive you."

"Get used to it. Anyway, it's for your own good. The first date can be so awkward, but this will break the ice."

"But I wasn't planning to go out with him at all."

"Kim, don't be silly. What point is there in meeting twenty new guys if you aren't going to try to get to know any of them better?"

"It wouldn't be fair to Dan. I mean, I really don't have any big attraction to him. Why waste his evening when it wouldn't lead to anything?''

"Maybe he wouldn't consider it a waste to have fun."

"At a school carnival? Riss—"

"And anyway, how do you know it won't lead to anything? You haven't given him a chance. He might be the nicest guy on the face of the earth.''

The argument was, of course, unanswerable. And it was too late to call Dan back and tell him she wasn't coming. Even if Marissa would give her his phone number from Brenna's list— which she probably wouldn't—he would already have left by the time Kim could place the call.

A school carnival, of all things....

She went to get her jacket and keys, and as she was coming back to the living room the doorbell rang again. "This place is turning into Grand Central Station," she muttered.

Tanner said, "You're the one who asked for it," and opened the door.

On the threshold, with his ever-present bundle under one arm and his smile fixed firmly in place, was Robert. His gaze slipped from Tanner to Marissa, already holding her purse, on to Brenna, seemingly asleep on the couch, and finally paused on Kim. "I called earlier," he said. "And someone told me you'd be home this evening."

"That was then," Marissa said firmly. "Sorry, Robert—the plan's changed. We're going out."

Robert's smile faded. "All of you?"

Kim felt sorry for him, but there wasn't much she could do. "Except for Brenna," she pointed out.

"Hey, Bren," Marissa said. "Here's your chance. If you're really nice to him, Robert might take pity on you and steam some broccoli."

At the sound of her name, Brenna stirred and opened her eyes. "The chef?"

Robert's eyes had glazed over. He looked, Kim thought, like a deer caught in the headlights of a car.

"Tell you what, Robert," Brenna murmured. "The heck with broccoli. Come sit next to me, and let's talk about fettuccini carbonara instead."

CHAPTER FIVE

ON THE way down in the elevator, Kim said, "Poor Robert. We shouldn't have left him like that."

Marissa shrugged. "All poor Robert has to do is turn the doorknob and leave. It's not like we left him locked in a cage with a man-eating tiger."

Tanner said, "Only a man-eating Brenna."

"She's not!" Kim's voice rose. "You've got her all wrong. Give her a chance. Brenna may be a little tactless at times, but—"

"I wish you'd choose a side and stick to it," Tanner said unsympathetically. "Are you worried about Robert or not?"

Kim bit her lip and decided that the only wise course of action was not to say another word to him all evening.

Not that he was going to notice that she wasn't speaking to him, she thought irritably, because Marissa instantly started talking about the carnival, and she kept it up until they arrived at the school.

The parking lot at St. James Prep was relatively small, and it was nearly full. As Tanner parked his Mercedes between a station wagon and a four-wheel-drive truck, Kim considered the narrow space on each side of the car and shook her head. "Are you sure you couldn't have found someplace tighter to park?" she asked. "Then there wouldn't have been any question about whether I could manage to get out of the back seat."

Tanner reached into the car, grasped her wrists and unceremoniously hauled her out. "You were saying?"

"Thanks—I think." Kim rubbed her wrists.

"There's Dan," Marissa chimed in. "He's waiting on the steps."

"Already?" Tanner asked.

Kim thought, *Is it so hard for you to believe that someone might actually be eager to see me?* But what was the point in saying it? She'd only look as if she was feeling sorry for herself.

She waved at Dan and hurried across the parking lot ahead of the other two.

"I've already got our tickets," he said, holding them up. "Want to go on in or wait for the others?"

"Wait," Kim said. "I suppose we'd better compare notes before we split up—see how long Marissa intends to stay, things like that."

"I'll take you home after the carnival, of course."

Kim was scarcely listening. Tanner and Marissa had stopped near the bottom of the steps. His head was bent, she was looking up at him, and as Kim watched Marissa smiled a little, said something Kim couldn't hear and laid a gentle hand on Tanner's shoulder.

The intimate gesture made Kim uncomfortable. *Watch out, Marissa,* she wanted to say. *Don't let yourself get drawn in. You're nothing like his usual sort of woman.*

But perhaps that was actually a good sign, she told herself. All the women she'd ever seen accompanying Tanner were the same type, and he appeared to go through them like popcorn. Maybe it would take someone like Marissa to make him realize what he'd been missing.

Or maybe he'd just break her heart—without ever realizing that unlike most of his companions, Marissa actually had one.

Not my business, Kim reminded herself. She'd warned Marissa once—that was absolutely all she could do. It was time to wash her hands of the situation.

She smiled up at Dan. "Come on. I'll buy you a lemonade or something."

The gymnasium was decorated as only a bunch of enthusiastic adolescent boys could imagine, with awkwardly twisted crepe paper streamers, overfilled balloons, and straggly lettered signs. Booths were scattered helter-skelter over the canvas which protected the floor from street shoes.

Off to one side, beyond a glass wall, was the swimming pool, and over it was rigged a collapsible stool hooked to a bulls-eye target. A sign on the glass invited everyone to take a shot at dunking the school principal for a dollar a throw. A line of boys waited their chance, and it appeared that at least a few of them had a pretty good aim, because the principal's hair was dripping.

"He's a good sport, to sit through that," Dan said.

"From what Marissa says, he seems to get along really well with the boys. Didn't you meet him at the party? She invited him, and I think he was there." Kim thought she recalled seeing the man once from a distance, but since it had been while she'd been trying to keep Tanner sequestered, she couldn't really remember.

Dan frowned. "I guess so."

"What's the matter?"

"Nothing. I just had to take a second look, since he looks different wet."

"That's for sure. There's a food stand." Kim pointed. "Oh, I should have remembered. This is an upscale, private prep school, so they don't have anything as ordinary as lemonade. Are you in the mood for espresso or an Italian soda?"

They carried their drinks along as they wandered from booth to booth. The parents' association was running a bake sale; Kim eyed the chocolate-chip cookies but decided that they looked too perfect to be homemade. Various clubs and organizations were showing off their skills. Here and there teachers had put up samples of their students' work, and at one end of the gym a brass quintet was tuning up, the tuba player showing greater enthusiasm than was actually necessary.

Dan seemed to be looking everywhere at once, as if he'd never seen anything quite like this. Kim watched indulgently, but by the time they'd made the second round of the gym, she'd lost most of her enthusiasm. "I think I'll sit down for a while," she said. "You go ahead and look."

Dan protested, but only feebly, and he soon went off to browse. Kim sat down near the bake sale booth and toyed with the dregs of her espresso, staring out across the sea of faces that filled the gym.

She didn't see Tanner until he spoke from behind her. "Thinking of calling a cab?" He pulled out a chair across the table from her.

"Not a bad idea. Dan might not notice I was gone for hours. Where's Marissa?"

"Manning the library club's booth. She told me to go entertain myself."

"Well, there's always the cakewalk."

"And what would I do with a cake if I won one?"

"Donate it back. That's how school carnivals really make money—by selling the same item a half-dozen times. I don't suppose Marissa had time to hit you up for a donation for the silent auction."

"You'd be wrong."

Kim shook her head in amazement. "Her devotion to the cause astounds me." She drained her espresso and tossed the paper cup into a nearby wastebasket.

"It's warm in here," Tanner said. "Want to get some air?"

She hadn't noticed, until he mentioned it, how stuffy the gymnasium was getting. Though a few of the ceiling-level windows were open, they were so far above the crowd that they didn't seem to be moving air at all. The mixture of smells—pleasant ones like chocolate and coffee, neutral ones like canvas, grating ones like chlorine from the pool—was making her head swim. "Sure."

Kim turned automatically toward the main door, but Tanner started off in the other direction. Down a short hall from the gym, in a half-hidden nook, he pushed open a door and cool outside air billowed through.

Kim eyed him speculatively. "Do you have a nose for the back exits? How did you know this was here?"

"Marissa told me."

Showed him, more likely. Kim shot him a sideways look, and thought he looked just a tiny bit self-conscious.

Though as far as that went, sneaking off to hidden corners—in school, no less!—to steal a kiss didn't sound much like Marissa. Kim had always thought she would be a little more careful than that of her job. On the other hand, Marissa wasn't in the habit of hanging around with men like Tanner Calhoun—men who could make sneaking off to a hidden corner an inviting prospect. At least not since Kim had known her...and probably not before that, either.

But she didn't challenge him. What difference did it make to her what Marissa and Tanner got up to? "I thought perhaps you went to St. James yourself."

"Was it here when I was thirteen?" Tanner didn't sound interested. He crossed the narrow concrete terrace and leaned on the steel handrail.

Kim followed, leaving a careful distance between them as she folded her arms on the rail. She looked out over the courtyard below, bathed in the glow of a full moon and quiet except for the soft strains of the brass quintet. The music had switched from a Sousa march to an almost hauntingly soft melody, trickling through the open windows of the gym and mixing with the soft air of the spring night.

"They should have set up a dance floor out here," she said. "What an atmosphere—my toes are twitching."

"Maybe that's why they didn't," Tanner said. "Talk about asking for trouble. A bunch of adolescent boys—throw in a few girls, and the last thing they need is atmosphere." He made a courtly half-bow. "But since we have the proper conditions and mademoiselle has twitchy toes— May I have this dance?"

Kim laughed and turned to face him. "Don't be absurd. I was only—"

"—Wanting to dance. I suppose the etiquette books would require me to go find Dan instead, but by that time the quintet will no doubt have gone back to Sousa and you'll have missed the chance." He held out his arms. "Come on."

It would be absurd to protest further—it was only a dance, after all, and would probably be a very brief one at that. But even as she moved into his arms, something deep inside Kim warned that she shouldn't do this. Shouldn't get so close to him. Shouldn't breathe deeply of the aroma of leather and aftershave. Shouldn't let herself like the feel of his shoulders under her fingertips and of his hands at her waist.

Shouldn't close her eyes and enjoy the sensation of moving in unison with him....

The music stopped, but for an instant she didn't realize that they were standing still, his arms still around her. She opened her eyes and found her face so close to his that she could feel the soft tickle of his breath against her cheek. It would be so easy to draw him a half-inch closer, to let her mouth rest against his....

What am I thinking? He's not my date, he's Marissa's!

Shocked, Kim planted both hands against his chest. ''I just remembered I need to check on the silent auction. The item I donated is a little odd, so I need to be sure they've marked it right.''

Tanner let her go so quickly that she felt even more like a fool. Had she thought he would hold her against her will? That he was so overcome with passion for her that he'd forget himself?

You are truly an idiot, Burnham. Talk about asking for trouble!

It seemed even warmer in the gym, after the soft outside air of the courtyard. But at least the heat would explain away any suspicious flush remaining in her face, Kim thought.

"The silent auction's set up on the stage," Tanner said.

She had been hoping that once back inside, he'd seek out Marissa and leave her alone. But he showed no inclination to leave her side. *So what's so odd about your donation that you had to come back in to supervise, Burnham?*

She almost tripped over a stack of books in the aisle between two rows of booths. A strange place to leave an obstacle, she thought, and took a closer look at the booth.

Three sides of it were bookshelves—the kind that folded up for storage or transport. Or at least, the booth had been nearly surrounded by bookshelves once; now one set of shelves lay on its side while another had collapsed forward. Both had spilled books wildly over the canvas floor. The third set of shelves was upright but empty—that must be where the books had come from which had almost tripped Kim. Marissa was holding the shelf steady, and Dan—whistling tunelessly—was tightening the screws which held it together.

"Hi, there," Marissa said breathlessly. "We had a little accident. When the boys built the booth they didn't get the shelves put together quite right, and they collapsed. Fortunately Dan kept this one from pinning me to the floor when it fell.''

"It's lucky he was here,'' Kim said.

"Darn lucky somebody was,'' Dan said. He shot a look at Tanner—a look that very clearly asked where he'd been when Marissa had needed assistance—and then went back to work.

Guilt pushed Kim into saying, "I'll help put the books back on the shelves, Marissa.''

Marissa shook her head. "It's all right. Just leave them where they are, because by the time Dan gets the bookcases all fixed, the carnival will be over. The boys can take everything back to the library tomorrow. Now don't hang around here, you're just getting in the way. Tanner, take Kim over to the cakewalk. If she wins, we'll all have dessert back at the apartment.''

"Try to win a chocolate one,'' Dan ordered.

Both irritated and chastened, Kim started off across the gym. *It feels as if we've been sent out to play,* she thought, and shot a glance up at Tanner, wondering if Marissa had any suspicion of what had happened out on the terrace.

Not that anything *had* happened, she reminded herself. It had been a fleeting thought, that was all—a momentary aberration. The sort of temptation that might strike anybody under those particular circumstances—finding herself surrounded by moonlight and melody, and in the arms of a very handsome man. Of course she'd been tempted. But she hadn't actually acted on that temptation.

And in any case, Tanner and Marissa had only had a couple of dates—it wasn't as if they'd announced a lifetime commitment. So even if she had kissed her roommate's date, there wouldn't have been anything exactly wrong about it.

Tacky, perhaps. Foolish, yes. Stupid, probably. Dangerous, definitely. But it wasn't like she'd have been doing something immoral.

So why was she feeling guilty?

Kim offered to ride home with Marissa and Tanner, but Dan insisted on taking her. He didn't exactly make her feel better, however, because for the entire drive he carried on a monologue about how self-centered Tanner had been not to be at hand to help when Marissa's booth had collapsed.

"She told him to go entertain himself," Kim pointed out.

"That's beside the point," Dan argued. "Of course she told him that, not because she wanted to get rid of him but because she didn't want him to be bored just standing around to keep her company. Still, he should have been there when she needed help."

"How was he supposed to know those bookshelves would collapse?"

"I saw how unsteady they were the minute I walked up to the booth."

"Well, that's a little different, don't you think? Naturally you'd see it—didn't I hear you tell Marissa that you work with wood all the time?"

"I'm a carpenter, yes. But anybody with eyes could have seen how wobbly those shelves were," Dan said stubbornly. "Besides, the point is he wasn't even there. He was off heaven knows where, doing heaven knows what."

On the terrace tempting me.

"And he wasn't even paying any attention to his date."

"Sort of like you right now," Kim murmured.

But the comment floated straight past Dan without making an impact. "What was that?"

"Nothing. There doesn't seem to be any place to park, but if you'll pull under the canopy by the front door, I can hop out."

"Aren't you going to invite me up for a slice of that cake you won?"

Kim eyed the brightly decorated box which held her prize, sitting at her feet. She'd been hoping to "forget" it in Dan's car.

"I would love to," she said mendaciously, "but I'd hate to have your car be towed just because you parked in the wrong spot."

"How about this one?" Dan swung his car into the last empty space in the lot.

Kim smothered a sigh. "I'll be darned. I must need to get my eyes checked. Do come up."

She'd already pushed the elevator button for her floor when Dan reached past her and grabbed the door to hold it. Kim was startled, until she saw Marissa and Tanner coming into the glass-walled lobby. "Wouldn't want them to miss out on the cake," Dan said, "since it was Marissa's idea and all."

In the living room of the apartment, Brenna was sitting in a yoga pose in the center of the carpet, arms raised above her head.

Kim noticed Tanner looking speculatively at Brenna, and she moved a step closer to him. "No bloodstains on the carpet," she whispered.

"But she looks pretty well-fed," Tanner said under his breath. "And I don't see a single sign of Robert."

Marissa eyed them both as if she'd like to scold. "How was your evening, Brenna?"

Brenna slowly lowered her arms and opened her eyes. "Quite lovely. Robert taught me to make low-calorie fettuccini carbonara."

Kim felt her jaw sag. "He *taught* you.... You *cooked?*"

Brenna stood up. "Or perhaps I should say that he demonstrated. But since I'm a very slow learner, I expect that the next dozen times I get hungry for fettuccini I'll need an additional lesson."

Tanner said softly, "I didn't think Robert was such a fast thinker. Feeding her carbonara to defend himself...the man's a genius."

The head offices of Westway Cosmetics were two suburbs closer to downtown Chicago than Printers Ink was, so Kim decided to drop off her final bid on her way to work rather than take the train all the way to the office only to turn around and come back in again.

She had never been to Westway before, and she was impressed. Everywhere she looked she saw the quiet evidence of a combination of money and good taste—from the deep-piled blue-gray carpets to the original watercolors on the walls to the lead crystal shades on the light fixtures. Nothing was ostentatious, but everything was first class.

And of course the people who had created this atmosphere would expect no less an effect from their next catalog. Kim held her briefcase a little tighter and thought for a wild instant about turning around and going straight to Printers Ink instead of continuing to trail behind her company escort down the winding hallway to the office of the marketing manager to submit her bid.

But it was the company who had set the specifications. It wasn't as if she was designing the catalog—only putting the ink on the paper. She had nothing to be afraid of. So she held her head a little higher and walked on.

She had her card ready, and when the marketing manager's secretary looked up from her work, Kim smiled and held it out. ''Kimberley

Burnham to see Ms. Wallace, with a bid for the new catalog.''

The secretary smiled. ''I'll take it, Ms. Burnham.''

A bit deflated, Kim fumbled as she took the glossy white folder out of her briefcase. She held it tightly for one last instant, feeling an irrational urge to kiss it goodbye, and then handed it over. ''If she has any questions—''

''I'm sure she'll be in touch,'' the secretary murmured. She put the folder on top of a stack of envelopes. It teetered and almost slid off, but she didn't notice; her gaze was already back on her work.

The door of the inner office opened, and a lilting soprano said, ''Thanks for delivering this yourself. We always appreciate the personal attention you give us.''

Tanner appeared in the doorway, pausing to shake hands with a statuesque blonde. Today he was wearing dark blue pinstripes—a suit Kim knew she'd never seen before—with a blindingly white shirt and a red tie.

The man must have a separate building to hold his wardrobe—a closet certainly wouldn't be enough. So all right, Kim admitted, she was feeling a bit of spite—and she had good reason.

Her bid landed in a careless stack on the secretary's desk, while Tanner's went straight onto the manager's desk?

So much for that competition. Why did they even bother to send out the specs?

"Good morning, Tanner," she said very deliberately.

Tanner turned. "Hello, Kim. It's a surprise to see you here. Don't tell me you're delivering a bid. Where is it?"

Did he have to make it sound as if she was incompetent? She didn't trust her voice, so she merely tapped a fingernail on the glossy white folder.

"Have you met Jerri Wallace? This is Kim Burnham from Printers Ink, Jerri."

Jerri Wallace seemed to be taken aback. "Your competitor?" She stepped forward to shake Kim's hand. "Very pleased, I'm sure. You have a bid for me, you said?"

Tanner took the folder off the pile and handed it to her almost carelessly. "Anything else, Kim?"

What's the point? "Oh, no," Kim said sweetly. "I don't want to take up your valuable time, Ms. Wallace—so I've put all the necessary information in the folder."

Tanner's eyebrows drew together slightly. "If you're on your way out, I'll walk with you."

"Oh, I'm certainly ready to go," Kim murmured.

"I'll see you next week, Tanner," Jerri Wallace called after them.

Kim's escort was waiting in the hallway. Obviously, she thought irritably, the man had known that she wouldn't be in the office long.

Tanner told him, "You can go back to your regular duties. I'll see Ms. Burnham out," and the escort smiled and faded away.

Kim waited till he was out of sight, then stopped in the center of the hallway. "Of all the unmitigated gall," she began.

Tanner looked astonished. "What did I do? If you're mad just because I'm walking you to the door—"

Kim shook her head. "No, though the mere fact that I'm required to have an escort while you're allowed to *be* one stings a little."

"Then what is it?"

"I shouldn't think I'd need to tell you. It's painfully clear that I don't stand a chance of winning that bid, no matter what the numbers say."

Tanner walked on a couple of steps. "You've got the same odds everybody else does."

"Everybody but you, maybe." She raised her voice from its normal alto, mimicking Ms. Wallace. "*We always appreciate the personal attention*—yeah, that sounds like a totally fair competition to me."

"Just because I know Jerri Wallace from college doesn't mean she's going to cut me any slack."

"But who makes the decision?"

"Jerri does—but she has a boss to answer to."

"Oh, that makes me feel *much* better. When I think how worried I was that you might have actually seen my bid on my desk yesterday.... You must have been laughing at the idea of me trying so hard to protect it."

He frowned. "I didn't see your bid, Kim. And if I had, I wouldn't have tried to read the fine print."

"Of course not—because you didn't need to."

"Let's continue this argument somewhere else," Tanner said firmly.

"I don't have anything else to say."

Tanner didn't answer. He strode off toward the main entrance, and Kim, with nothing better to do, trailed after him.

Outside, he stopped beside his Mercedes. "I'll take you back to the train station."

"Don't put yourself out."

"Get in the car, Kim." He opened the door.

"Oh, why not? I might as well save myself the walk."

He slid behind the wheel and started the engine. "You're saying that I'm conspiring with my friend the marketing manager to get the job even if my price is way out of line."

"I'm sure you have that covered, the same way you got the Pettigrew account. *Perhaps my bid is better in other ways,*" she quoted. "There must be something in there that Jerri Wallace can point to as worth the extra costs, in case her boss starts asking questions."

"That's a pretty strong accusation, Kim— and I don't like having my honesty questioned any more than you would."

That was true, and the reminder stung Kim like a hive full of honeybees. "Sorry," she said finally. "I jumped to conclusions, and I'm sorry."

Tanner put the car in gear. "Wait and see how it turns out," he said. "We'll probably both be underbid by some upstart who thinks owning a photocopy machine makes him a printer."

Kim couldn't quite let it go. "You have to admit it looked bad, though—all the other bids land in a stack on the secretary's desk while yours is hand-delivered straight to the woman who'll make the decision."

"My bid was in the same stack as yours. I handed it to the secretary and she said Jerri wanted to see me. About another matter entirely, I might add."

No surprise there, Kim thought. She wondered how hard Jerri Wallace had had to look for an excuse.

"Are you headed to work?" Tanner asked.

"Yes. Why?"

"Then I'll take you there instead of to the station."

"You don't have to."

"It's not exactly out of my way, Kim."

"In fact, it would be less bother for you to drop me at Printers Ink than at the train station."

He shot a glance at her. "As a matter of fact, you're right, though it's not very genteel of you to comment on it. Besides, why stand on the platform and wait, when you can be all the way to your office by the time the next train pulls in?"

She couldn't exactly argue with that. So she settled back into the leather seat and made up her mind to enjoy the treat.

"So how did you enjoy your evening with Dan?" Tanner asked.

"He seems to be a nice young man."

"Strike Dan from the list."

"What do you mean?"

"Calling him a *nice young man* sounds like the kiss of death for a relationship. I thought—speaking of kisses—that you didn't look terribly enthusiastic when he asked you to walk him to the elevator last night."

And exactly what business is it of yours? Kim wanted to ask. It was entirely beside the point that he was right—Dan had kissed her goodnight with more zeal than finesse. She'd been quite happy to get back into the apartment—even though the first thing she'd seen when she walked in was Marissa sitting on the arm of the couch next to Tanner and laughing at something he'd said.

"One down, twenty-some to go," Tanner murmured. "Who's next on your list? Have you organized them from most to least likely, or are you going to eliminate the obviously impossible ones first? I'm not counting Dan in either category, you understand, since that date last night was a bit of an aberration."

"If you don't mind, I really don't feel like discussing my dating plans with you."

Tanner shrugged. "Whatever you say. But if you need advice anytime—"

"I'll certainly keep that offer close to my heart. In the meantime, I'll give *you* some advice. You might watch out for Dan."

"He's out to get my hide?"

"I don't know. But he was acting awfully protective of Marissa."

"Was he, now?" Tanner murmured as the Mercedes pulled up in front of Printers Ink. "Well, don't fret about me keeping an eye on Marissa. Are you planning to bid on that job for Hallowell and Sons?"

"Of course not. You know I can't print four-color fast enough to do that project."

"Yes," Tanner said. "I just wasn't sure whether you knew it."

Kim bit her tongue hard to keep from asking whether he was really saying that she couldn't handle the Westway job, either. What did it matter? She wasn't going to get a chance to prove what she could do—not as long as Jerri Wallace was the one making the decisions. She got out of the car and slammed the door.

The window slid down, and Tanner leaned across the seat. "It's too bad," he went on, "because we could have made a date of it and gone together to drop our bids off. Oh, I forgot—my name was crossed off your list long ago, wasn't it?"

He grinned at her, and the Mercedes pulled smoothly away.

CHAPTER SIX

IF TANNER ever had been on her list of desirable men, Kim fumed, that last comment would certainly have wiped him off it. Not because his idea of a romantic date was going together to turn in bids for a job, because she knew perfectly well it wasn't. Except, perhaps, where Kim was concerned. If it had been any other woman he'd been thinking of....

Don't dwell on it, she told herself. *His entire object was to knock you off balance, and the longer you fuss about it the more successful he's been.* If Tanner knew the way she was stewing about this, it would probably make his entire day.

As she pulled open the door of Printers Ink, Marge looked up from her desk just inside the entrance. "You're late," she said. "Rick's been looking for you. He had a question about a job."

"The Tyler-Royale direct mail circular?"

"I don't know which job it was. He didn't tell me the details, he just hovered for half an hour until I finally told him I'd send you back to see him the minute you hit the door.''

''Let me drop my briefcase first.'' Kim set it on her desk and pulled off her raincoat.

When she came back out of her office, Marge eyed her trimly cut dark rose suit. ''New outfit? What's the occasion?''

''Seeing the marketing manager at Westway Cosmetics.'' That had been the original intention, anyway, and there was no need to explain to Marge what had actually happened. Kim was irritated enough without having Marge fueling the flames with her own resentment.

''I thought maybe you put it on especially for your ride in the Mercedes.'' Marge looked up over her half-glasses. ''Couldn't help seeing it pull up in front. Since when is Tanner Calhoun running a taxi service?''

Kim grinned. ''Thanks for the idea, Marge. Next time I'll offer him a tip.'' Feeling immeasurably better, she opened the door behind Marge's desk leading back toward the pressroom.

''Don't get ink on that suit!'' Marge called after her.

The pressroom was relatively quiet for the middle of the morning. The Ripley press was methodically thwacking away at the employee newsletter Tanner had brought over, which was due across the street tomorrow morning. The pile of printed pages was growing slowly but steadily.

But the larger presses were quiet, and around the corner of one of the machines, Kim could see a shock of white hair where Rick, the head pressman, was bending over to adjust something. "Having trouble?" she called.

He straightened up, rubbed the small of his back for an instant, and laid his wrench aside. "No, just fine-tuning while I was waiting for you."

"What's the problem?"

"Have you heard anything about the copy for the Tyler-Royale direct mail ad circular? It hasn't come in yet."

"Well, it isn't due any particular day."

"I know. They're unpredictable at best. But in the meantime that job for St. James school is waiting. Their student handbook, remember? But if I start printing those and then the ad copy comes in, I'll have to stop midway through the run."

Kim nodded. "And if you have to interrupt the job and then set the press up again later, we take the chance that the handbooks won't all look quite alike.''

''I don't know how pernickety the school's likely to be. But I know that when that ad circular comes in, Tyler-Royale will want the finished project right away. So do I sit and wait for the circular, or work on the handbooks?''

''Start the handbooks,'' Kim said. ''Even if there's a minor variation from one handbook to the next, it's not going to be enough that the ordinary person will notice. Nobody's going to be comparing them side by side, anyway.''

''You gave the school quite a price break, didn't you?''

''Yes—though that wouldn't excuse giving them less than our best work. But they do understand that because they're getting a bargain, the handbook has to be fitted in around all our other work.''

''And maybe in the next week or two we'll be busier than we've ever been before,'' Rick said, ''and mighty glad to have at least one nuisance out of the way. All right, I'll start running them this morning. How did the bid-letting go, by the way?''

Kim sighed. ''Well, I don't think any of us should spend the bonus money just yet.''

"Not very promising?"

"Not encouraging at all."

"Damn," Rick said. "I was looking forward to that job. At first I thought you were nuts to go after it, but it would stretch us a little and let us show what we can do. Haven't had that kind of a job since..." His voice trailed off.

"Since the partnership broke up," Kim finished for him. Her voice was level. "You've never mentioned those days before."

"Maybe it's time. It'll soon be twenty-five years, you know. You weren't much more than a baby when it happened."

"I was four years old."

Rick shrugged. "That's what I said—a baby. I was only a punk kid then myself, just starting to learn the trade."

Kim pulled up a tall stool. "Why did you decide to stay with my father instead of going with Charles Calhoun? Or did they draw straws to see who went and who stayed? I've always been curious about that."

Rick shrugged. "I have no idea what went on in the head office, except that sometimes you could hear the yelling all the way back here, even with the press running. But I stayed because your dad came and asked me to. He asked all of us, actually, but a couple of the other guys were excited about starting something new, so they couldn't wait to move on. It ended up being just me and the head pressman who stayed. Now he's long gone and here I am in his place."

"Being head pressman is something of an empty title around here these days," Kim said. "I was hoping the Westway job would change that—let me hire a couple more people at least so you could supervise instead of running the press yourself all the time."

"Ah, maybe it's better this way," Rick said. "Less pressure. We were risking a lot on that one job."

Kim appreciated the effort to cheer her up, even though Rick's words had been more comforting than the underlying tone of his voice. No question about it, he was as disappointed as she was.

Of course, nobody could win every job they bid on. But it was a lot easier to accept the ups and downs of the profession if the selection process was fair. And in this case...

Look ahead to the next one, Kim told herself. *Cut your losses and move on.*

*   *   *

The Bachelor Bazaar had certainly accomplished its main purpose—their phone was ringing off the wall. Kim happened to be the first one home that evening, and it took fifteen minutes just to play back all the messages. Most were for Brenna, which was no surprise to Kim. But Marissa had a respectable number as well, and Kim herself had gotten a couple of calls. One was from Robert, which made her feel bad all over again for having abandoned him to Brenna on the previous evening. Making dinner for her—the guy was a phenomenally good sport.

Brenna came in while Kim was still writing down phone numbers. She flipped through her own stack of messages and set them aside.

"You aren't going to call any of them back?" Kim asked.

"Of course not. Haven't you any idea how to play the game? Never respond to the first message, and be no more than lukewarm about the second call. By the third time a guy calls—"

"I'd think a lot of them would give up before the third call."

"Not if they're worth having." Brenna went down the hall to her bedroom.

Kim ignored Brenna's advice and returned Robert's call, listening to the background noise of an obviously busy kitchen while she waited for him to come to the phone. "I don't want to keep you from work," she said hastily when he finally answered, his voice sounding rather gruff. "But you didn't exactly say what you were calling about, so I thought I should get in touch right away."

"Nice of you to do that," he said, sounding both surprised and pleased. "I thought I might stop by with dessert after work. If it's convenient, that is."

Smart move, Robert, Kim thought. *You've learned to call first, to be certain who's going to be here.* "I'm not intending to go anywhere tonight." Perhaps, however, a warning was in order. "I think Brenna and Marissa will be home, too."

Brenna strolled through the living room just in time to hear, and she shook her head. "Not me—I'm meeting the stockbroker that came to the party with Marissa's friend Eve."

Kim put her palm over the phone. "Has he called three times already? How did I miss hearing about it?"

"I'll see you in a few hours," Robert was saying. "Our special dessert is crème brûlée, tonight. It's best just as soon as it comes out of the oven, and it won't keep overnight."

The chef might not be altogether tactful, Kim thought, but he was funny. "We'll be happy to help you out by cleaning up the leftovers, Robert."

Robert sounded abashed. "That wasn't what I—"

Kim laughed. "I know it wasn't. And trust me, crème brûlée doesn't show up so frequently around here that we ask many questions about its origins. See you later."

"Crème brûlée?" Brenna said. "It's a good thing I'm going out, because crème brûlée is far too much of a temptation."

"Maybe Robert has a low-calorie version," Kim offered.

Brenna rolled her eyes and picked up her jacket. "See you later. Have an extra bite for me."

"You mean you're not making the stockbroker pick you up here? I thought that was one of the rules, too—not making things too convenient for your date."

"Well, this isn't really a date, just a drink," Brenna said. She was gone before Kim could inquire about the exact distinction between the two.

She'd barely put the phone down when it rang again. Since she expected it was Robert calling with a forgotten question, she was still smiling as she answered.

"It's downright amazing," Tanner said, "what a nice voice you have when you're not being suspicious."

"It all depends on who I'm talking to."

"Are you still mad at me?"

"I wasn't exactly mad at you," Kim pointed out. "I was disgusted, yes. But I wasn't angry."

"Well, good—I'm glad we got that all cleared up. So you're manning the phone at Dating Central tonight? How did that happen? Did you draw the short straw, or have the three of you set up a regular rotation?"

"It only happened because in a moment of insanity I forgot why we have an answering machine. Why don't you call back and I'll let you talk to it?"

"Because you're more fun."

"But I'm a lot less reliable," Kim warned. "In fact, I feel a lapse coming on even as I reach for pen and paper. *Marissa—Tanner called to say he doesn't want to see you again, ever.* No, wait a minute. This one is even better. *Tanner called to propose to you.* Or maybe I'll leave both messages for her and let her figure out what you really meant to say."

"As a matter of fact, I wasn't calling to talk to Marissa."

Kim opened her mouth and shut it again without making a sound. That was the last thing she would have expected.

"I'm calling for two reasons, actually. One is to ask if you'd like to be on the board of governors of the industrial park. I'm on the nominating committee this year and my fellow committee members came up with your name."

I might have known it wasn't your idea. "No, thanks. I'm too iconoclastic for boards and committees."

"A rebel who refuses to rubber-stamp decisions can be really valuable."

"Or just a darned nuisance."

"That, too. But before you decide, perhaps you should take your time and think about it,

Kim. You'd be missing an opportunity to influence the policies of the entire area.''

''All right,'' Kim said agreeably, ''I'll keep it in the back of my mind for a day or two, and then I'll say no. What was the other reason you called?''

''I'm looking for Brenna.''

''You want to talk to the man-eater? Incredible.''

''You said yourself I should give her a chance. I'm just doing what you told me to.''

Kim decided to ignore the bait. ''I wonder what Marissa will say about this development.''

''Ask her if you like.''

Kim shivered at the very idea. ''Brenna isn't here at the moment—actually she's out on a date—but I'll leave her a message.''

''Just ask her to call me.''

''I feel I should warn you,'' Kim said sweetly, ''that she makes it a policy not to return phone calls from prospective dates. Not till the third call, at least—so you might want to start counting.''

''Care to make a bet on whether she'll call me?''

''You don't really want to risk it, Tanner. If the stakes were worthwhile, I could simply not give her the message. Then of course she wouldn't call, I'd win the bet and—''

''And the next time I see her and ask why I haven't heard from her, you'll be in big trouble with both of us. What are you willing to wager, Kim?''

''You really mean it? All right. How about that cappuccino we never managed to have?''

''That's so very dull and pedestrian of you, my dear—you disappoint me. You know, you sound awfully insecure about your own convictions, if a cup of coffee is all you're willing to put on the line. Surely you're willing to risk something more interesting than that.''

''More interesting in what way? If you're expecting that I'll do something completely crazy like offer to sleep with you—''

''Now that sounds more like it. Done.''

''I didn't mean—'' Kim heard her voice start to rise and stopped herself in midsentence. Tanner was joking, of course—he didn't want to sleep with her any more than she wanted to sleep with him—so there was no reason for her to feel panicky. But if she didn't treat the matter with a lightheartedness that equaled his own, Tanner might start to wonder if there was some hidden reason she was taking such a kooky bet so seriously. He'd be wrong—but the question would still be uncomfortable. It would be far better to go along with it, especially since she'd win, anyway—she could count on Brenna for that.

"Sure," she said. "Why not? Only we haven't exactly established the terms."

"What's to decide?" Tanner murmured. "It's perfectly clear. If I win, you sleep with me. If you win, I sleep with you. Good night, Kim—pleasant dreams!"

With Brenna out for the evening and Marissa unaccounted for, Kim found herself thinking longingly of the carnival the night before. The entertainment level might have been a bit sophomoric, but at least it had been unpredictable— which was more than she could say of the very boring book which lay open on her lap. She yawned and wrapped her grandmother's wedding-ring quilt more tightly around her.

It was getting late. Robert's restaurant must be unusually busy for a Tuesday evening, and it appeared that Brenna's stockbroker had turned out to be extraordinarily exciting. As for where Marissa was... She only hoped Marissa got home before Brenna did. Though Kim wasn't looking forward to telling her about Tanner's call, it would be a whole lot better than having her find out from Brenna.

Kim was almost asleep when a key clicked in the lock, and she was startled when Marissa came in with Robert, who was cradling a very large insulated paper bag. "Look who I found in the elevator," Marissa said. "Robert says you were expecting him."

Kim tried to untangle herself from the quilt so she could get up, with little success.

"Sit still," Robert ordered. "I'll just take all this through to the kitchen."

"One thing about it," Marissa mused. "Coming home is a lot more adventurous these days. You never know who you'll run into." She sank onto the opposite end of the couch from Kim. "I hate school board meetings—especially ones where I have to make a presentation. These little talks are supposed to be simply to inform the board, but let's be realistic—these are the people who are setting the budget for next year, so if they're not impressed…"

Better say it fast, Kim thought, before Robert came back and there wasn't another opportunity. "Riss, Tanner called tonight."

Marissa yawned. "What did he want?"

Kim took a deep breath and plunged. "To talk to Brenna. I thought you should know."

Marissa sighed deeply.

"Sorry," Kim mumbled. She didn't know what else to say.

Robert returned with a tray held high. "Crème brûlée for everyone," he said. He set the tray on the coffee table. "Dig in."

Kim was feasting her senses on the perfect brown crust atop the custard dishes. "We couldn't be so inelegant as to gobble something that looks like this."

Marissa reached for a spoon. "Speak for yourself. I'm famished after that incredible meeting."

Robert pulled up a straight chair and sat down across from them.

"Aren't you going to have one?" Kim asked.

He shook his head. "I eat far too many rich dishes at work. I thought you said Brenna would be here, so I brought three."

"Oh—when you called she was just going out."

"She's home now," Marissa murmured.

Her ears must be more sensitive, Kim thought, because the first thing she herself heard was Brenna's key turning in the lock a moment later.

Brenna paused in the doorway. *Making an entrance,* Kim thought.

"Having a party without me? Shame on you," Brenna said cheerfully.

Robert sat up straighter. "I brought one for you."

"Lovely man," Brenna murmured. "But I can't, really."

Marissa spooned up the last bite. "Tanner called while you were gone, Bren. He asked for you."

Kim was startled. But perhaps Marissa felt it would be easier to accept the fact if she said it out loud herself.

Brenna blinked, and then smiled. "I wondered how long it would take him to get around to it," she said. "The silly man. I wouldn't have thought he was too shy to ask directly. Did he leave a number?"

Kim gaped at her. "You're not going to call him back, are you?"

"Well, there are exceptions to the rules," Brenna murmured. "But you're right—it would only feed his ego."

Kim relaxed. "You had me going for a minute there."

Brenna sat down and absentmindedly picked up the remaining crème brûlée dish. "And Marissa's already done enough ego-boosting to make him difficult to handle, without me adding to the problem."

Kim watched with interest as Brenna dug her spoon into the rich custard and closed her eyes to savor the first bite. She'd never seen the woman indulge herself in a dessert before.

Suddenly Brenna seemed to realize what she was doing. "Naughty of you, tempting me like this," she told Robert. "I hope you realize the trouble you've caused with that fettuccini lesson last night."

"Trouble?" Robert said faintly. "I thought you liked it."

"I did. That's the trouble. I told these two how good your fettuccini is, and they want me to show them how to make it."

Kim glanced at Marissa, who shook her head—obviously denying that she'd told Brenna anything of the sort. It seemed time for some defensive action. "Actually," Kim said, "I think it would be more useful to learn directly from the master."

Brenna dropped her spoon and snapped her fingers. "That's it. We'll have a dinner party. Robert will teach us all how to make some gloriously special dish, and everybody can pitch in with the work and enjoy the results. Let's see— there are the three of us and Robert, so we'll need two more men to keep the numbers even. I'll invite Tanner, and we'll find someone for you, Marissa." She grinned at Kim. "What an idea, Kim—thanks. You've given me the perfect excuse to call Tanner back. Where's his number?"

The scent of ink which had been freshly laid on paper was one of Kim's earliest memories. As a toddler, she'd had an endless supply of scratch paper, drawing and coloring on the backs of pages which had been rejected because they were smeared or unevenly printed. And she still found herself taking a deep, almost nourishing breath the moment she walked into the pressroom—or indeed, into the Printers Ink building.

Her fondness for the aroma of fresh printing was one of the reasons that she never minded pitching in to help in any area except running the press itself. Not only was Rick protective of his territory, but truly understanding the intricacies of that job would require years of hands-on experience—so Kim didn't fiddle with the presses. Everywhere else, however, she could pitch in—and often did.

She was in the shipping room, helping to sort the student handbooks for St. James Prep and shrink-wrap them in bundles of a hundred, when Marge poked her head in. "Tanner's in the front office," she said. "I told him you were busy, but he said he'd wait."

"I wonder what he wants." There surely wasn't anything wrong with that first employee newsletter he'd passed along to her, or he would have been sitting on her doorstep as soon as the finished product was delivered, not a few days later.

And he certainly wasn't calling to collect on his bet, either. In fact, Kim hadn't caught a glimpse of him in the two full days since Brenna had phoned him, crème brûlée dish still in hand and Robert still sputtering beside her, to invite him to dinner on Sunday evening.

Which goes to prove, Kim thought, *that I was right—he was only yanking my chain when he made that bet.* He'd been teasing when he'd jumped on her accidentally suggestive suggestion. And he must have been a little disconcerted himself to get such a quick response. To have his bluff called, in a sense.

There was some satisfaction, Kim decided, in having caught the man off guard and not quite sure how to act—even if it had been more Brenna's doing than her own.

Kim left her shipping clerk finishing up the last of the bundles and returned to the main office. Tanner was sitting on the corner of Marge's desk, swinging one foot as he talked to her.

Kim gave a handful of student handbooks to Marge. "Samples for the files," she said. "What can I do for you today, Tanner?"

"I thought perhaps you'd like a ride over to Westway for the bid results. Jerri did call to tell you she's announcing her decision this afternoon, didn't she?"

"Yes, but I wasn't planning to go," Kim said crisply. "There didn't seem to be any reason to spend a good part of yet another afternoon on a job I won't be getting anyway."

"Being a poor sport isn't going to win you any points. And there's something to be said for visibility as well. It's the salesman who comes back over and over who eventually makes the sale.'' Tanner's voice was lazy, as though he were going through the motions rather than really trying to convince her.

''He can't sell anything,'' Kim said, ''no matter how many calls he makes, if the customer has already bought from someone else.''

But he did have a point, Kim admitted. The main reason she'd wanted to present her bid to the marketing manager in person was so Jerri Wallace would remember her the next time Kim bid a job, and therefore be more likely to give her the work. It was human nature to hesitate to work closely with strangers, to trust them with large projects or sizable sums of money.

And if nothing else, listening to Jerri Wallace explain her decision would help Kim figure out whether there was any point in ever again bidding a Westway job.

Besides, she was intrigued with the question of why Tanner was there. And why—if he really wanted her to go—didn't he sound more convincing?

''Oh, all right,'' she said. ''I'll go through the motions. But you don't have to provide limo service.''

Tanner consulted his watch. "If you're going to be there in time, I'd better."

"So thoughtful of you not to want me to be left out." Kim went to get her jacket.

He helped her into the car in a little more personal a fashion than he had before, and Kim felt wariness creep over her. As he slid behind the wheel, she said, "So what's really going on, Tanner?"

"Quick on the uptake, aren't you?" He started the engine. "I didn't think you'd like it if I discussed our bet in front of Marge. Brenna called me, you know."

"And so you're wondering when I intend to pay off?" The man was smooth, Kim had to give him that much. "Well, that's easy enough. I'm not going to."

"Cheat," he said, but his voice was calm.

"Not at all. In the first place, I didn't lose—because Brenna didn't exactly return your call. She phoned you with an invitation, and that's a different thing altogether. Just ask Brenna—she'll tell you."

"You don't really want me to call her up for clarification."

"Why not? Unless you'd feel uncomfortable talking to a woman you're dating about going to bed with someone else—and heavens, if you're thinking about *doing* it, I don't see why *talking* about it would bother you."

"I thought perhaps it would bother Brenna," Tanner murmured.

"Not likely. She has an enlightened attitude about these things."

"So you think she'll take your side."

Kim felt a tickle of uncertainty deep inside. Was he being entirely too agreeable about this? "Yes, I do."

"All right. In that case, I lost the bet, and I'll pay up whenever you like."

I should have seen that one coming, Kim thought. It was past time to call a halt. "Fine," she said crisply. "Would you like to climb in the back seat right now?"

"Of course," Tanner said easily.

Kim's stomach turned over at the thought.

"But there is this inconveniently timed bid-letting," he went on.

Kim nodded. "That's true—and I'm sure you wouldn't want to explain to Jerri Wallace why we were arriving late and disheveled."

"Disheveled? Kimberley, honey, I love it when you get suggestive."

She had completely lost track of where they were, and she was startled when he pulled the car into a slot in Westway's parking lot. It was a good thing she hadn't been the one behind the wheel, Kim admitted, because as shaken up as she was, they'd likely have ended up in the middle of nowhere.

Since she was with Tanner, the receptionist at the front desk didn't summon an escort for Kim but instead waved them both down the hall toward the marketing office. It was a detail that felt like salt in the wound to Kim.

The waiting room outside Jerri Wallace's office was nearly full of people. Tanner nodded to the secretary and pointed to the last two chairs. Kim sat down and said under her breath, "All these people put in bids to print the catalog?"

"Plus a dozen or so more—some from out of town—who aren't here this afternoon." Tanner didn't sound as if the matter concerned him much.

"Well, that will make you feel especially good when you get the job," Kim murmured.

"Kim, nobody's rigged this contest."

"Of course not." She picked up the closest reading material, which turned out to be Westway's current catalog.

They had no sooner sat down than the secretary picked up the telephone and murmured a few words into it. Then she raised her voice. "You can all go in now."

"It's not rigged, you say," Kim said softly. "And I suppose you also expect me to believe it's pure coincidence that this shindig starts within thirty seconds of you getting here."

Tanner shrugged. "I always had excellent timing."

Next door to Jerri Wallace's office was a meeting room with chairs set up in rows. As the crowd settled down, an almost-concealed door opened and Ms. Wallace came in with a folder in her hand and took her place at the lectern. "This was a difficult decision," she began.

"I'll bet," Kim muttered.

"The bids were very close this time—in fact, they fell within just a few cents per unit in many cases. And we had some interesting proposals which incorporated new ideas, including one from—let me see—Printers Ink, which was actually the next-to-lowest figure. In the end, however, we've gone with a bid which was not only the lowest by a few cents but one we've worked with before—Calhoun and Company. Congratulations, Tanner.''

''What a surprise,'' Kim said coolly. ''Amazing—just a few cents difference.''

''You can't still think I snooped on your desk, Kim.''

Kim fixed him with a stare. ''I don't think you had to, Tanner.''

''Thank you all for coming,'' Jerri Wallace continued, closing her folder. ''I hope you'll continue to consider our business. We will of course continue to consider all of you.''

The group began to file out, but Tanner turned away from the door. ''May I have a moment, Jerri?'' he called.

The woman didn't stop, but she nodded and left the door into her office open.

''Come on in, Kim,'' Tanner said.

''Oh, no. You can't expect me to listen to you arrange the details without blowing up. Much better if I go sit in the waiting room.''

His hand closed on her elbow. ''You may find this instructive.'' He closed the door after them. ''Jerri, you remember Kim Burnham from Printers Ink. I wonder if I can look at the two lowest bids.''

''Yours and hers?'' Jerri paged through the folder. ''It's not exactly standard practice, but I suppose if Ms. Burnham doesn't mind...''

Kim shrugged. ''I don't see why—but go ahead.''

Tanner sat down in one of Jerri Wallace's deep chairs and spread Kim's carefully arranged bid across his knee.

Jerri leaned against the corner of her desk. ''Sometimes we have to humor Tanner,'' she murmured. ''But since I have the opportunity to ask—I loved that suit you were wearing the other day. Is it a designer model?''

''Not exactly,'' Kim said. ''It came off the rack at Tyler-Royale. We do a lot of work for them—direct mail advertising pieces and that kind of thing—so I shop there whenever I can.''

''I'll check it out. Thanks.''

I'll bet, Kim thought, eyeing the careful cut of Jerri Wallace's dress. But at least the woman was tactful.

Tanner tossed the proposal onto the corner of Jerri's desk. ''Those new ideas from Printers Ink you mentioned are fabulous,'' he said. ''If

I were you, Jerri, I'd look again and change my mind. Kim's bid is a few cents higher, but it's a better deal for you. You should throw out my bid and take her up on it.''

CHAPTER SEVEN

KIM'S ears were ringing. Had Tanner really told Jerri Wallace what Kim thought she'd heard?

It's a better deal for you. You should take her up on it.

She couldn't be hearing right. Tanner Calhoun could not possibly have just handed her the biggest job she'd had in the last five years. And not just any job, but one that he'd won—perhaps not quite fairly and squarely, but definitely won.

Kim's bid might be a few cents higher, but it's a better deal for you.

Why on earth hadn't he simply taken the business and run?

She caught a glimpse of Jerri Wallace from the corner of her eye and noted that the marketing manager looked every bit as startled as Kim herself felt. That reaction confirmed what Kim had already concluded—this wasn't normal behavior for Tanner. He didn't habitually win a bid and then talk the client out of hiring him. Not that he could stay in business long if he did—but Jerri Wallace's stunned face made it clear that this behavior was unprecedented.

So why had he done it?

Jerri reached for the two bids. "I'll definitely look them over again." Her voice sounded thready, as if somebody had kicked her in the stomach.

And perhaps she felt that Tanner had just done exactly that, Kim thought.

There might not have actually been any shenanigans to make sure that his was the winning bid. Perhaps he'd legitimately come in lowest, without so much as a hint from the marketing manager about what his competition was offering. Without even taking a glance at the proposal lying on Kim's desk. Without any fiddling with the numbers to make him appear the lowest bidder even if he really wasn't.

Still, Jerri Wallace had felt it necessary to justify her decision to the assembled bidders by explaining that she'd chosen Tanner not only because his price was lowest but because their previous dealings assured her that he could handle this new challenge equally well. And then he had turned right around and tried to give it away.

Did he not want the job after all? And if so, why not?

"I'll be in touch no later than tomorrow with my final decision," Jerri said.

Tanner nodded. "Take your time. Let's go, Kim."

As if she were operating on autopilot, Kim shook Jerri's hand and left the office. They were all the way to the parking lot before she found her voice. "What's wrong with the job, Tanner?"

He closed her car door and walked around to slide behind the wheel. "Why do you think there's something wrong with it?"

"Because you suddenly don't want it anymore."

"I never said I didn't want it."

Kim shook her head. "Oh, no. What you did in there just now—you don't want the job, or you wouldn't be trying to pass it off on me. A few days ago, you wanted it badly enough to spend precious time coming up with a price— and trust me, I know exactly how long it takes to figure out all the details in order to get a bid right. Now you're trying to get rid of it. So what changed your mind?"

"I'm not trying to get rid of it, Kim."

She was barely listening. "You aren't doing this out of philanthropy. You aren't running the Red Cross or the Salvation Army, holding out a helping hand to someone in need...." She paused to think. "Or maybe you *are* doing it for charity," she accused. "Poor little Kim needs all the help she can get, so we'll sacrifice a job here and there to keep her going."

"That would be no way to run a business. If my motive was charity, I'd have told Jerri exactly what I was doing, and why."

"No, you wouldn't. She couldn't help but think her business was pretty unimportant to you, if you'd give it away to anybody who came along just because you felt sorry for them."

"You're hardly just anybody, Kim. I certainly wouldn't put my own credibility on the line by telling her you can do a better job than I can—not unless I believed it. If I did, and you screwed it up, I'm the one who would look like a fool."

"And heaven knows we can't have *that,*" Kim said. "All right, then. You say you aren't passing the job along because you feel sorry for me. But what other reason is there?"

"You can do a better—"

"Right," Kim said. "Though as a matter of fact, you didn't look at it long enough to tell for sure whether there was any real difference at all."

"Perhaps I knew what I was looking for, so it didn't take long."

"Or perhaps you were just putting on a show. Of course, instead of giving jobs to Printers Ink in order to keep me going, it would be smarter for you to eliminate the competition altogether."

"If I want to get rid of you, Kim, why would I be passing on work to you?"

"That's different—getting those small jobs out of your hair increases your productivity and your profits and impresses your clients at the same time by showing how much you're willing to put yourself out to accommodate them. You aren't doing it because it's good for me, only because it's good for you."

"Of course, there's always the possibility that it could be good for both of us."

There was a hint of suggestiveness in his voice that stopped Kim cold. *It could be good for both of us....*

"It's business we're talking about here, Tanner," she snapped. "Not sex. Unless you think that I'll feel such overwhelming gratitude to you for giving me this job that I'll fall into bed with you after all.''

Tanner shrugged. ''You're the one who set the terms of the bet. I was just being agreeable.''

''And now you're trying to change the subject. Why? Because I was getting too close to the bone? Maybe I hit it right on the head, and that's exactly what you're doing, Tanner. You're eliminating the competition. Perhaps you think I can't pull off the job, and you're convinced it'll bankrupt me when I fail—and then you won't have to deal with me at all anymore.''

''Why are you so certain I must have a reason? Other than the obvious, of course, which would be that I actually believe that you put together a better package.''

''Because you don't think that way. It has to be one or the other, Tanner. You're either convinced I can't do it and failing will bring me down altogether, or you've just figured out you don't want the job at the price you gave Jerri. Which is it? Did you suddenly remember that you forgot to factor in some major cost? Maybe you got interrupted while you were working the bid, and you forgot about overtime wages, maybe. Or perhaps it was something like paper. Maybe you bid the job for twenty-pound paper and only when it was too late you realized that Jerri had specified sixty-pound.''

''I know perfectly well what the paper specs are, Kim.''

''Then it's something more subtle.''

He shot a look at her and said gently, ''Oh, absolutely. Just think about how fond Jerri will be of me when she realizes that I put Westway's best interests above concerns for my own profits.''

''Oh, you've got all the sides covered—I admit it. Still, if you could make money at that price, you wouldn't be trying to dump the job on me while you pretend to be doing it out of the goodness of your heart.''

Tanner shook his head. ''You are one incredibly suspicious female, you know that?''

''And exactly when did this problem occur to you? While you were sitting outside Jerri's office this afternoon? Or earlier? Maybe that's why you dragged me along in the first place—because it dawned on you, after it was too late to withdraw your bid, that you'd messed it up on a grand scale. So, knowing you couldn't take the bid if you won it, you wanted a backup plan. If Jerri Wallace had awarded the job to someone else, you'd have given a big secret sigh of relief and invited me out for coffee. But she gave it to you, so you had to get rid of it somehow. That's why you made up a fairy tale about how my offer was better—''

He took both hands off the steering wheel and started to applaud.

Kim glared at him. ''Would you watch where you're going?''

''I am watching. I'm just not steering at the moment, because I'm too busy giving credit to the best piece of fiction I've run into in months. Maybe you're in the wrong end of the printing business, Kim. You could write fantasy with the best of them.''

''Whatever the reason is, if you'd just admit it so I know what I'm dealing with—''

''There's nothing to admit.'' When the Mercedes slid to a halt at a stoplight, Tanner pulled a cell phone from his belt. ''Fine. I'll call Jerri right now and tell her I was having a moment of temporary insanity and I'll be happy to take the job.''

Kim gritted her teeth. *He's bluffing,* she told herself. *He won't call her.*

And yet... What if he was telling the truth?

"What's it going to be, Kim? Are you so sure of yourself that you'd turn down another chance at the job?"

Was she willing to blow the biggest opportunity she'd had in her five years at Printers Ink?

Wrong question, she thought. *Am I willing to blow Printers Ink by trusting Tanner Calhoun?*

"I want to look at your bid," she said stubbornly. "You looked at mine—now I want to see yours."

"It won't be anything you haven't seen before."

"It wouldn't be fair not to let me compare the differences for myself."

"To make sure the extras you threw in are actually worth the few cents more you asked for? Or to reassure yourself that you're not the one who offered the moon and only now realizes that you'll be paying a big price for it?"

"A little of both," Kim admitted.

He took his eyes off the road to stare at her. "Surely that isn't uncertainty I hear in your voice, Kimberley. Or—no, it couldn't possibly be humility, or regret that you made accusations that might not be true." The Mercedes pulled up in front of Printers Ink.

Kim didn't move. "You have to admit that I have good reason for being suspicious, Tanner. After all the years—"

"Do you mean all the years when your father and my father couldn't get along? That was them, Kim. This is us." He leaned across her to open her door. "Let me know when you've thought it over."

There was a stack of messages waiting for him—there nearly always was, when Tanner had been out of the office for a couple of hours. But he ignored the slips of paper on his desk and stood by the window, arms folded, looking across the street to where the slanting rays of late-afternoon sunlight warmed the bricks of the Printers Ink building and turned them to a deep purplish-red.

Perhaps, he thought, he should have left well enough alone. Perhaps he should have kept his mouth shut, and kept the Westway job. But it was too late for regrets now—it was done.

He wasn't surprised that Kim was dubious of his motives. She had good instincts, even if this time they happened to be wildly misdirected.

And he didn't exactly blame her for being suspicious, either. Ben Burnham and Printers Ink had definitely come off the worse after the partnership broke up. Tanner didn't know whether that was sheer chance or if his father had done some manipulation to keep his former partner from achieving the kind of success Calhoun and Company had. Frankly he didn't want to know. He'd told Kim once that what had happened back then didn't matter anymore, and he firmly believed what he had said.

He wondered if she would ever agree.

Kim had plenty of time to think that afternoon. The school handbooks were waiting to be picked up, Tanner's employee newsletter was long finished and delivered and the copy for Tyler-Royale's direct mail advertising still hadn't come in.

Over the years, she had gotten so used to the roars and thumps of a press operating at full speed that she scarcely heard it anymore—until it stopped. Then, the silence seemed even louder. It echoed painfully against her eardrums, reminding her that if the presses weren't running, no money was coming in.

And today the silence also reminded her that the biggest job of her life might be waiting for her after all. *If* Tanner hadn't changed his mind, called Jerri Wallace and convinced her not to take a second look at Kim's bid after all.

Why, Kim asked herself, had she pressed him so hard?

Because, she thought stubbornly, it still didn't make sense that he'd have simply given her the job like that. There had to be a reason— and unless she found out why he'd been so eager to get rid of the Westway catalog, she couldn't be certain she wouldn't fall straight into the same trap.

But in the meantime, she'd better concentrate on her real business. Like the Tyler-Royale direct mail advertising circular.

She phoned the department store's advertising division and asked for the woman she usually worked with. ''She's out sick today,'' the woman's assistant said. ''I don't know anything about the circular, but I'll look around and see if I can find anything. And I'll leave a message for her to call you when she gets back.''

Knowing it was the best she could do for the moment, Kim left her number and hung up. She told Rick he could take the rest of the day off,

but he shook his head and announced that he
needed to adjust and clean the Ripley press anyway and a slow afternoon was just the time to
do it.

In the front office, Marge was working on
the books. "It makes me nervous when things
get so quiet around here," she said as Kim
walked through.

"We have slow periods every now and
then," Kim pointed out. "They tend to be followed by very busy ones." *Like printing the
Westway catalog.*

But she wasn't certain enough of that yet to
mention the possibility to Marge. If she did, and
it didn't come through after all…

She went back into her office, and she was
pricing out a job for another regular client when
she heard the fax machine behind Marge's desk
buzz and then begin to spit out paper. *The
Tyler-Royale circular,* she thought in relief. *The
assistant must have found it.*

Marge wheeled her chair around, picked up
the sheaf of paper, and brought it into Kim's
office. "I think the folks across the street have
their fax machine programmed wrong," she
said. "It looks like this should have gone to a
client instead of coming here. Want me to send

it back, or just call and tell them they hit the wrong speed-dial number? Though I don't see why they'd have our number in their fax machine in the first place.''

Kim took the pages, hardly believing her eyes as she looked. Tanner had actually faxed her his bid for the Westway catalog?

''No, it's supposed to be here,'' she said. She hardly recognized her own voice.

Even when she'd asked Tanner if she could see his bid, she hadn't held more than a faint hope that he'd actually allow her so much as a glimpse. To tell the truth, she'd have been happy to get a quick look, the same kind of brief scan that he'd given her bid in Jerri Wallace's office. But for him to actually send her a full copy....

She could study it at leisure, comparing every last condition and term and price to her own. More importantly yet, at least in the long run, she could figure out his thinking. She could deduce how he set his prices. And she could use that knowledge next time—in fact, every future time—they went head to head.

Kim admitted that it was probably not the most ethical use of secret business information. Still, he'd given it to her of his own free will.

It wasn't as if she'd burgled his desk in the dead of night, or picked his pocket, or paid off someone in his office, or traded personal favors for a secret copy.

Unless he expected her to offer those self-same personal favors in return, in gratitude for his generosity....

Don't even think about that stupid bet, she told herself.

''Marge, would you make a fresh pot of coffee?'' she said. ''I'm going to be tied up for a while.''

As soon as Marge left, Kim got out her copy of her own bid and put the two side by side on her desk. She would compare them line by line, item by item, penny by penny.

She was barely getting started when the bell above the front door rang, and she glanced out to see a tall man in a dark blazer and khaki trousers come in. He looked familiar, Kim thought, as he paused for a second beside Marge's empty desk, then looked around and came toward Kim's door.

She felt like grabbing her papers and crawling under the desk so she wouldn't be disturbed. Instead, she stood up. ''May I help you with something?''

"I got a call that the handbooks for St. James Prep are done, and I'm here to pick them up."

No wonder she'd thought she should know him. "You're the principal," Kim said. "I didn't expect you to pick them up yourself."

He shrugged. "We all wear numerous hats at St. James. Depending on the time of day, I'm receptionist, substitute teacher, basketball coach, janitor. Just now I'm the delivery man."

"Yes, Marissa has mentioned that everybody there is multitalented. The handbooks are back in the shipping department. Did you park out front?"

"Around the side of the building, actually."

"Good, that will make the boxes easier to load." Kim led the way through the building.

"Thank you for the compliment, by the way."

Kim frowned a little.

"About being multitalented," the principal prompted.

"Oh, of course. Marissa's always telling me about school. I don't know how you manage it all—so many boys, all at such a difficult age."

He grinned. He had quite a nice smile, Kim noted. "Sorry I didn't get a chance to talk to you at the carnival," he said. "Or at your party, either. I tried, but you seemed quite occupied that night.''

''Oh—at the party?'' Kim tried to sound vague. ''It was quite a mob, wasn't it? I'm surprised you even noticed I was at the carnival—there were so many people. And you were pretty busy, getting dunked and all.''

''It's my job to keep one eye on everything—even when both of them are full of water.''

Kim laughed and pushed open the door to the shipping department. ''Here are the boxes. I'll go look for Rick to help you carry them out.''

''Kim,'' he said, and there was a tentative note in his voice that made her turn around in surprise. ''I wonder—could I buy you dinner sometime, as a small thank-you for doing this work for us?''

Kim laughed. ''Oh, if it's to be a gesture of thanks for the handbooks, you should probably invite Rick instead of me. He's the one who did all the work.''

The principal didn't join in her amusement. ''I just thought perhaps you'd go out with me sometime.''

Wrong move, Kim. Now the question was how to repair the damage. "I'm sorry," she said soberly. "I didn't mean—"

He nodded. "I should have been more specific. How about dinner tonight, and not because of the handbooks?"

Kim hesitated. Yet there wasn't any real reason to refuse. She had no plans for the evening—other than puzzling out the psychology behind Tanner's bid and his behavior. And hadn't this been the original goal of the Bachelor Bazaar in the first place—simply getting to know a few more people, without pressure?

"That would be nice," she said, and fled to the pressroom to find Rick. She sent him to the shipping department to help load boxes of handbooks, and retreated to her office, closed the door, and put in a panicky call to the apartment. She closed her eyes in relief when Marissa answered on the fourth ring, just as the answering machine kicked on.

"Boy, I'm glad you're home from school early," Kim breathed. "Because your principal just asked me out for dinner—*and I can't remember his name.*"

*   *   *

Gregg—the principal—took Kim to a German restaurant in the Loop, and over sauerbraten and a nice Rhine wine, they discussed St. James Prep, the shortage of qualified teachers and the general state of education in the city. The evening was pleasant enough, but the conversation seemed to limp from topic to topic, and Kim found herself struggling to find things to talk about. She supposed that was largely because she was so concerned about putting her foot in her mouth again, as she'd done when he first invited her.

Why, she asked herself in utter frustration as she watched him demolish a slice of Black Forest cake, had she ever come up with the idea of the Bachelor Bazaar in the first place? And, having once thought of it, why hadn't it occurred to her that the whole thing was likely to feel unnatural, calculated, even a bit manipulative?

You didn't beg him for the invitation, she reminded herself. *Dinner was entirely his own idea.*

Still, she felt oddly guilty—as if she were hiding something. She'd had similar feelings when Marissa had conned Dan into taking her to the school carnival, and when poor Robert had gotten stuck with Brenna for an entire evening.

If the guys had known what they were getting into when they'd accepted the invitation to the Bachelor Bazaar, Kim thought, it might have been a little different.

But it was too late for that. The best she could do to avoid future discomfort—for herself and for the men in question—was to turn down all future invitations from men who had been at the party.

Or else, she supposed, she could confess what had really been going on that night. Unfortunately such openness might turn out to be unpleasant all the way around. Brenna, Marissa, and the other women who'd been involved no doubt wouldn't appreciate having the whistle blown on them at this stage. And there was simply no way to predict which of the men they'd invited would be amused by the idea of the Bachelor Bazaar and which ones would feel they'd been hung up on a butcher's rack like slabs of meat waiting for inspection.

Tanner had not only figured it out for himself but he'd seemed to be amused. On the other hand, she suspected that Dan and Robert would feel they'd been exploited, if they ever found out.

She looked across the table at Gregg and wondered which category he fell into. He'd seemed to have a sense of humor—for surely a man without one wouldn't have agreed to spend an evening in a dunk tank as the target of a bunch of adolescent boys. And yet her feeble joke this afternoon about inviting the pressman to dinner instead of her had certainly fallen on barren ground.

It was only an idle speculation, of course, for Kim had no intention of experimenting. Not just now, at any rate—and not with Gregg. Better to learn from the experience, cut her losses and remember not to make the same mistake again.

There was at least one good thing about the whole mess, she thought dryly. Unlike giving up chocolate-covered caramels or kettle corn, swearing off bachelor bazaars wouldn't be a hard resolution to keep.

Gregg finished his coffee, paid the bill and mused that school mornings came early. With a flood of relief and feeling glad not to have to make an excuse, Kim agreed that she, too, needed to be at work on time tomorrow.

The valet brought Gregg's car around, and Kim relaxed in the passenger seat. For a man in a hurry to get home, she thought, he was certainly dawdling along Lake Shore Drive. Every other car in sight was sweeping past. He seemed as if he had something on his mind but was reluctant to say it.

Gregg turned into the parking lot of Kim's apartment tower, and she gathered up her handbag. "You don't need to walk me upstairs," she said. "At least one of my roommates will be there."

"I was just thinking about that," Gregg said. He pulled the car off to the side, but not into a parking spot. "Why don't we just go to my place instead?"

Kim was puzzled. "But you said yourself it's getting late. Surely you don't want to drive all the way back downtown to bring me home again tonight."

"Not at all," Gregg said, and smiled. "Stop being coy, Kim. You know what comes next. Why bother your roommates when we can have complete privacy at my place?"

Kim's muscles seemed to freeze. "If you're implying that dinner is necessarily followed by a romp in the sack—"

"That's the game, Kim. Everybody does it."

Was the harsh note that had crept into his voice new, or had she simply not paid any attention before? "Well, I don't," she said coldly, and pushed the door open.

Gregg's hand closed on her arm. "That was a very expensive dinner, Kim."

Kim stared him down. "I'm honored that you value my services so highly."

For the first time he seemed to hesitate, and his grip loosened. "I didn't mean...well, I didn't mean that."

"I don't care what you meant. I'll send you a check for my dinner. Now if you don't mind..." She pulled away and slammed the car door.

She was still steaming when she reached the apartment. The first thing she saw was Marissa, who was feeding the goldfish in the aquarium.

Kim shut the door and leaned against it. "We are never again going to do anything so stupid as the Bachelor Bazaar," she announced. "However, I wish to go on record as saying that our original criteria were not specific enough. We should have added *sensible*. And *sensitive* wouldn't have hurt, either."

Marissa's eyebrows went up. Her gaze slid past Kim and on toward the kitchen.

Sitting on a tall stool at the counter, laying out a game of solitaire, was Tanner. "Did something go wrong with the date?" he asked pleasantly. "You know, I'm still crushingly curious about what the qualifications were for being included in the Bachelor Bazaar. If *sensible* and *sensitive* weren't on the list, what in the heck was?"

"What are *you* doing here?" Kim screeched. "Brenna's working tonight!"

"I came to see you."

"Oh, now that's a nice excuse. Dating three women in the same apartment—what an efficient arrangement!"

"I didn't say it had anything to do with dating." Tanner moved a card and flipped over the top three from the pack. "It happens to be the literal truth—I came to see you, not ask you out. Marissa told me you were on a date but would be home soon, and she invited me to wait."

Kim shot a look at her roommate, who merely shrugged. Marissa seemed to be perfectly at ease with the idea, Kim thought. *Or else she's every bit as good an actress as Brenna is.*

"Now I'm very glad I stayed," Tanner went on. "What happened? Did he stick you with half the dinner tab? No, that would come under the heading of sensible, and you said he wasn't."

Kim flung herself down on the couch. "I'm not talking to you about my date, Tanner."

"All right," he said calmly. "I'll change the subject. Did you have fun taking my bid apart this afternoon and trying to figure out where I'd fouled up?"

Kim admitted, "I didn't find anything obvious."

"That's because there wasn't anything."

"Is that why you came tonight? To ask what I thought of the bid?"

"No. I came to tell you that Jerri Wallace called me earlier. She said she'd tried to get you at the office but you'd already left for the day."

Kim's heart skipped a beat. "And the verdict?"

The silence stretched out as Tanner moved several cards. Kim, who wanted to sweep the whole array off the counter onto the floor so it would stop distracting him, controlled herself with an effort.

"If you want it," Tanner said deliberately, "you've got yourself a job."

The biggest job of her career had dropped into her lap, courtesy of Tanner Calhoun—and Kim didn't know whether to be delighted, terrified, or dubious about it. She settled for being watchful and wary, and spent a nearly sleepless night trying to anticipate everything that could possibly go wrong with the job. The list was so long she didn't even get obsessive, because instead of dwelling on the first few snags she'd come up with, she kept thinking of new ones.

As soon as she arrived at the office the next morning and found the message from Jerri Wallace asking her to call, Kim did some intense deep-breathing exercises, looked once more at her own bid and Tanner's and picked up the phone.

"I've reconsidered the proposals," Jerri told her, "and based on Tanner's recommendation, I'm offering you the job—if you're still interested."

Kim flipped a mental coin and tried to keep her voice steady. "Yes. I want it."

''Then I'll fax you the contract immediately. It's right here on my desk, so you can expect it within minutes. As soon as you've faxed it back, I'll send the camera-ready copy over by courier. According to your proposal, you can have the finished product to us within ten days. I'll be counting on that. And Kim—remember this. I'm going out on a limb, hiring an unknown to do this project. Don't disappoint me.''

Or you'll regret it till the day you die. Jerri didn't have to say the words, Kim thought. They hung in the air anyway.

She put the phone down, waited for the fax, scrawled her name in a fashion that was much less steady than her usual signature and handed it to Marge to fax back to Westway. Then she went back to the pressroom to tell Rick that the long shot had paid off after all.

And found him huddled on the floor next to the Ripley press—pale, sweaty and shaking, gasping for breath and barely able to speak.

CHAPTER EIGHT

KIM stood frozen for an instant, staring at Rick, unable to believe what she was seeing. He couldn't possibly be curled up on his side on the concrete floor, helpless and in pain. Rick was indestructible.

She leaned into the shipping room next door and told the clerk to call an ambulance. Then she dropped to her knees beside Rick to assess his condition as best she could.

What she found most terrifying was not the grayish shade of his face or the obvious pain in his eyes but the fact that he didn't protest at the idea of an ambulance. That wasn't at all like the Rick who came to work even when he had the flu. The man who had actually, years ago, limped around the pressroom for weeks on crutches because he'd broken an ankle playing racquetball. His fellow employees had even joked that Rick was so devoted to Printers Ink that he'd scheduled his gall bladder attack for a week when he was on vacation.

"Are you having chest pain?" she asked crisply.

Rick shook his head and gasped, "No—it's not my heart, it's my back." Instead of his usual deep baritone, his voice cracked and wavered.

Well, that's good news. At least, I think it is. "Just lie still," she ordered. "Can you tell me what happened?"

"I was leaning...into the press." He could manage only a few words at a time. "Adjusting the tension...something gave way."

"You mean a muscle in your back snapped?"

"No, a part of the press. I had my weight braced on it."

"So when it broke it threw you off balance and you fell?"

Rick nodded. "Hit my back on the corner of the press. Landed on the concrete, hard." He tried to shift his legs and winced. "I think I heard something crack."

"Don't move," Kim ordered. "The paramedics will be here soon."

She stayed beside him while the ambulance crew stabilized him. When they tried to lay him on his back, Rick screamed, and Kim wanted to shriek right along with him. When the ambulance pulled away, she went back to the office and sank, shaking, into her chair.

On her desk blotter lay the Westway contract, where Marge had laid it—which meant the receptionist had already faxed it back to Jerri Wallace. And sending off that signed sheet of paper meant the clock had started ticking. Kim had ten days to produce the new Westway catalog—and no pressman to do the work.

She felt like banging her head on the nearest wall.

When it came right down to it, of course, she was far more concerned about Rick than about the catalog. The crack he thought he'd heard when he fell sounded plenty ominous to Kim, and the few words she'd gotten out of the paramedics hadn't been reassuring. But Rick was on the way to the hospital, and he would receive the best possible care. He wasn't her responsibility just now.

At the moment, she wished she could say the same about the catalog.

The little bell above the front door jingled. From her desk, Kim couldn't see the doorway, but she could see Marge's face, and she watched as it turned into a stolid mask. There

was only one person on earth, in Kim's experience, who could make Marge look like that—
but she was supposed to be on a cruise ship in
the Caribbean.

The steel-under-velvet voice of Letha
Burnham murmured a perfunctory greeting as
she bypassed Marge's desk and came straight
to the door of Kim's office.

Kim stood up, preferring to meet trouble
head on. ''It's a surprise to see you here, Letha.
Wasn't the Caribbean sunny enough to suit
you?''

Letha sat down, crossing her slim legs and
arching one foot to show off her stiletto heel.
''I didn't go on the cruise—though I can't
imagine you're surprised that I felt I had to sacrifice my vacation. After the way you were carrying on last time I was here—''

Kim ran her mind back over the past ten
days. Of course, that was it—Tanner's phone
call and Letha's visit had coincided. Talk about
bad timing.

''I've been looking into things ever since,''
Letha said.

''It was a phone call, Letha. Why should that
prompt a full-scale investigation?''

"Because the Calhouns never did anything without a reason. This one is more charming than most, but that doesn't mean his motives are any better."

More charming than most... "You've talked to Tanner?"

Letha's gaze shifted. "Only a little."

That's why he's feeling sorry for me, Kim thought. *Because he's encountered Letha.*

But that didn't fit with the conclusions she'd reached yesterday after examining his bid for the Westway contract. He hadn't given her the job out of pity. Yes, it had been generous of him to step aside when he'd already won the bid. But he'd actually been right when he'd told Jerri Wallace that Kim's offer was the better one.

Still, did his blithe explanation of how he'd benefit by looking like the good guy really hold water? Compared with doing the work himself, and making the profit....

She tugged herself back to the moment. "What have you found out, Letha?"

"Not a great deal. That's why I haven't been in to see you before. But I'm here now to give you a warning. Don't trust him. He's out to get something from you. I'm still trying to find out exactly what it is.''

She swept out without another word. Also, Kim noted, she left without asking for another advance against the profits she insisted were owed to her—and that, as far as Kim was concerned, was far more troubling. If Letha was agitated enough to forget about money...

She thought it over for a while. *He's out to get something from you.* Letha might just possibly be right. On the other hand, Letha's perceptions were often colored by her unique sense of what the world—and Kim in particular—owed her.

One thing was certain, Kim concluded. If Tanner *was* out to get something, he was in a pretty good bargaining position at the moment—even if he didn't yet know it.

Because—just as soon as she got her breath back—Kim was going to have to walk across the street and beg.

The atrium lobby at Calhoun and Company was every bit as beautiful as Kim remembered it. The yellow canary was in equally good voice. The flow of water in the fountain was just as relaxing—or at least, Kim thought, it would

have relaxed her if her business had been anything less important.

She hadn't called for an appointment, and the
receptionist, the same one who had shown her
into the conference room on her previous visit,
blinked once in what looked like well-
controlled astonishment before he phoned
Tanner to tell him she was there. He looked
equally startled at the answer he got, Kim
thought. At any rate, he put the phone down
abruptly, as if it had suddenly grown hot, and
stood up. "I'll show you to his office," he said
and led the way.

They walked past the closed door of the conference room that Kim remembered so well,
and at the end of the hall the receptionist tapped
on a door, pushed it open and stood back for
Kim to enter.

Tanner's office occupied the corner of the
building which most easily overlooked Printers
Ink, just across the street. Kim wondered if the
precise location had been his idea or if he'd
inherited the office space—and the view—
along with the business when his father retired.

He was standing by the window when she
came in. "Thank you for seeing me so

quickly,'' she said. ''I'm sorry to intrude like this.''

''I spotted you coming across the street.'' He gestured toward a pair of chairs in the corner. ''And it's no intrusion. I'm glad to see you.''

There was a soft note in his voice which made Kim's throat tighten. He sounded as if he really meant it—as if he'd actually been looking forward to seeing her. But that led to questions she wasn't sure she wanted to ask.

He's out to get something from you. Letha had been thinking in terms of business, Kim knew. But was it possible it was much more personal than that?

Tanner sat down across from her and said, ''I have another job for you.''

Kim wanted to laugh—but she couldn't decide whether the desire rose from amusement at her own crazy thinking or simple hysteria. Of course it wasn't personal. How could it possibly be personal? The man was dating both of her roommates, for heaven's sake.

''I was going to bring it over this morning,'' Tanner went on. ''Then I saw the ambulance and figured you had your hands full. Is everything all right?''

"More or less. But I do have my hands full. Right now I can't take on another thing."

"The job can wait a few days at least. But I haven't even asked why you're here. Surely you didn't come to deliver anything as commonplace as an apology."

Kim bit her lip. "Not exactly. Though I do regret the things I said yesterday."

"Which ones, precisely, are we talking about?"

Did he have to make some sort of game of it? "All of them," Kim said irritably. "I'm sorry I said that you were giving me the job out of charity, and that you were trying to duck out of doing it yourself, and that you plotted to stick me with it so I'd be ruined. Have I missed anything?"

"Those are the main ones I remember. And you're actually apologizing for saying them?"

"Yes." She sighed. "Though as far as that goes, if you had been trying to bankrupt me, you couldn't have come up with a better scenario than the one I'm stuck in right now."

"Really? Would you like a cup of coffee while you tell me your tale of woe?"

She nodded, and while he was at the small coffee cart in the corner of the office, she told him about Rick. "The paramedics said that of course they couldn't tell anything without some tests," she said, gratefully taking the cup he handed her. "X rays and things like that, I suppose. But they suspect he fractured a vertebrae, because he was in too much pain to have just sprained something." She sipped the rich brew. "And as far as that goes, even if it turns out to be just a pulled muscle, he won't be able to run the press for days."

Tanner sat down again, cradling his own cup in the palm of his hand. "Without him, you can't handle the Westway catalog." It was not a question.

"That's about the size of it. I'll have to back out of the job."

"You can't," Tanner said coolly.

"Don't you hear me? Without Rick, I'm out of business."

"That was careless of you, Kim—relying on one individual to that extent."

"Maybe it was," she admitted. "Perhaps you can afford redundant layers of staff, but I can't. I've done the best I can to cover—I can do every job in the building myself, except Rick's. In a pinch, I could probably even run the Ripley. But I can't do it as well as Rick can. And on a job like this one... I don't have any option but to pull out.''

''You'll kill any chance of ever working with Jerri again.''

Her voice rose. ''Do you think I don't realize that? Look, Tanner, this is already difficult enough without you rubbing salt in the wound.''

''I didn't intend to—only to make clear the extent of the problem.''

''Oh, sure. Like I haven't already realized the extent of the problem! I've thought it over, and the best thing I can do is to admit right away that I can't produce. It would be even worse if I tried to muddle through and ended up giving Jerri Wallace a bad job.''

''That's true.'' Tanner rubbed a forefinger along his jaw. ''She'd never forgive you for that.''

''I know. That's why I'm here to beg you to take the job back. At least that way when I call Jerri I can give her a solution, not just dump a problem in her lap.''

''There are alternatives.''

''Like what?''

''I'll loan you someone who can run your press.''

Stunned, Kim sat and stared at him, unable to believe what she had heard. She must have misheard, she thought, since Tanner didn't appear to think he'd said anything out of the ordinary. He was drinking his coffee as calmly as if they'd been discussing the weather.

''Why would you do that?'' she asked finally. ''I've handed you the chance to destroy Printers Ink—why would you rescue me?''

''Because I don't want to destroy you, Kim.''

''Oh, right,'' Kim said dryly. ''I'd forgotten. I come in very handy for those nuisance jobs you don't want.''

''That's not my reason. More coffee?''

Kim shook her head. ''No, thanks. I have no idea what you're talking about, you know.''

Tanner went to pour himself another cup. ''I believe that breaking up the business all those years ago was a mistake.''

''But what has that got to do with—''

''And I think we should put it back together again.''

Kim almost dropped her cup. ''You mean renew the partnership?''

''I was thinking more of Printers Ink becoming a division of Calhoun and Company.''

"You want to buy my business," she said slowly.

"That's not exactly what I have in mind, either. I'm thinking more of a merger."

"I'm not sure I understand."

"If I simply wanted to offer the kind of work you do so well, I wouldn't need Printers Ink— I could just buy equipment and start up a new line. I have the space, and I can get the manpower. But the fact is I don't want something else to supervise."

"You want me to do it instead."

"I want you to keep on doing it," he corrected. "A good bit of the value of Printers Ink is you, Kim—so unless you're part of the package, I'm not interested."

Kim's brain was still reeling.

"There would be advantages for both of us, you know," Tanner went on. "You'd have access to staff and resources you can't afford now, and you could specialize without worrying so much about the overhead. I'd be able to promote those small but unique jobs, instead of trying to avoid them."

"Without worrying about whether you could pass them off to me—because that would be my job. I'd be working for you. Answering to you.''

"In a sense, I suppose. Face it, Kim, you hardly have the assets to negotiate a position as a full partner."

"No," Kim agreed. "That's why I'm here this morning in the first place. Is this all connected somehow?''

"Connected?''

"Yes. If I don't agree to your proposition to buy me out, you'll withdraw the offer to loan me the help I need."

Tanner didn't answer, but he looked intrigued at the idea.

Kim could have kicked herself. He might have already thought of that little twist, but just in case he hadn't, why had she had to go offer it to him on a silver platter?

"Is that the way you'd operate?'' he asked. "No, the two things aren't connected. It just seemed a good time to bring up the merger idea.''

"When I'm down and out," Kim muttered.

"Down, perhaps—but out? Not you. Take your time and think about it—but I'll loan you the pressman no matter what." He set his cup down and walked across to his desk to pick up the phone. "Harry, can you spare one of your guys for a week or ten days?"

Kim caught herself biting her thumbnail.

Letha had been dead right after all. Tanner *was* out to get something from her.

It appeared that he wanted darned near everything she had.

Even though the dinner party had been Brenna's idea in the first place, it was Kim and Marissa who staggered through the supermarket on Sunday afternoon, loaded down with everything on Robert's list.

Marissa juggled an armful of fresh greens so she could check the list once more. "I think that's it, finally. Unless you think we should get the arugula instead."

"I'm going to hang Brenna for getting us into this," Kim announced.

"Be a sport. Shopping is the worst part. And just think of how luscious dinner will be." Marissa eyed the beef tenderloin Kim was cradling. "It will be worth it. Beef Wellington and chocolate mousse—what else could a woman want?"

Kim didn't bother to answer. "Who did you decide to invite?"

Marissa dropped the greens onto the check-out counter. "Dan."

"Dan the carpenter? Well, that should make things even more interesting. Dan took me to the carnival, but tonight he's your date—while Tanner took you to the carnival, but now he's with Brenna. Of course poor Robert is still stuck in the kitchen, but at least this time he won't have Brenna breathing down his neck." She set the tenderloin down next to the vegetables and began to unload her arms of cans and bottles. "Maybe after dinner we can play a few rounds of musical chairs."

Marissa looked puzzled. "Musical chairs? Why?"

"It just seems to fit the ambiance of the party. Or perhaps spin-the-bottle would be even more appropriate."

Marissa looked appraisingly at her. "You're certainly in a rotten mood, Kim. What's the matter? It's not like you to be so awfully cynical."

What *was* the matter with her? Kim didn't know for sure, but there were plenty of possibilities.

She was sympathetic with Robert and annoyed for his sake at how Brenna had manipulated him in order to have an evening with Tanner. On the other hand, nobody had forced Robert to take part, so perhaps he didn't really object to the idea of the dinner party after all—and in any case, that was Robert's problem, not Kim's.

She was still on edge about the Westway catalog, of course. Chris, the pressman who had reported for duty less than an hour after Kim's talk with Tanner, seemed to know his business well enough. At least the press had been humming along at what seemed an incredible speed, and pages were piling up in every corner of the pressroom, waiting to be assembled, folded and trimmed. Still, Kim couldn't help but think about what would happen if they didn't make the deadline.

She was worried about Rick, who was still in the hospital and who seemed perfectly content to stay there for a while. Though all the tests showed that he hadn't actually fractured any bones, his doctors weren't talking about when he might be able to return to Printers Ink. And even when he came back, Kim knew, he wouldn't be working at his usual pace, or tossing around cases of paper and barrels of ink as he'd been in the habit of doing.

She was wary of Letha Burnham, who had been calling her regularly. Kim hadn't told her about Tanner's offer of a merger, and she had no intention of doing so. No matter what Letha thought, what happened to Printers Ink was Kim's decision.

And of course she was uneasy about the whole idea of a merger. She couldn't lightly give up control of a business her father had worked so hard to build. If she did, she felt she would somehow diminish the value of his work, of the years he had struggled to keep Printers Ink going after the partnership broke up. She couldn't easily give up her independence and start answering to someone who just a couple of weeks ago had been a fierce competitor, if not exactly a bitter enemy. But on the other hand, Tanner was right about the advantages. If Printers Ink were to become a division of Calhoun and Company, she wouldn't have to worry about hiring some muscle to help Rick. She wouldn't have to fret about cash flow, or be quite so watchful of where the next job was coming from.

''Hello?'' Marissa's voice held a tart edge. ''If you're going into a coma, Kim, it might be

smart of you to lie down *before* you lose con-
sciousness.''

Kim shook herself. ''Sorry. I didn't mean to
drift off like that.''

''So what's the matter?''

Robert. Westway. Rick. Letha. Tanner....
''Only the usual stuff.''

''Right.'' Marissa pulled out her credit card,
swiped it through the reader and made a sour
face as she signed the receipt. ''Brenna had better pay her share, that's for sure. Since this was
her idea in the first place.'' She started to gather
up bags. ''You're absolutely sure it isn't man
trouble?''

Kim was genuinely puzzled. ''Man trouble?
Of course not. Oh, I feel a little guilty over
Robert, since he didn't exactly ask me for this
date. But—''

''Well, this isn't really a date tonight for any
of us.''

''I suggest you don't tell Brenna that,'' Kim
said dryly, and hailed a cab.

''She doesn't think Tanner's really serious
about her.''

''I hope not, because if she does, she'll be
disappointed. Just as you were.''

Marissa sounded intrigued. "Did you really think I was upset?"

Kim thought it over as they piled into the cab and tried to arrange the bags so they could sit comfortably. Had the woman lost her mind? "Well—yes. You mean you weren't?"

"Just remember what I said," Marissa murmured. "This isn't really a date tonight for any of us. It's just a bunch of friends getting together for dinner."

By the time they got back to the apartment, Robert had already arrived. His knives and utensils were laid out in a surgical-looking array, and he was donning the huge, all-enveloping apron that the tools had been wrapped in. Brenna was sitting on one of the tall stools beside the serving counter arranging tulips and daffodils in a low vase.

"Just in time," Robert said with satisfaction, and started to unpack the bags. "Were you able to get everything on the list?"

"I hope so," Kim said. "It feels as if we bought everything in the store."

"Hey, shove over," Marissa told Brenna. "Leave some room up here for the food."

"You shouldn't disturb an artist at work," Brenna said without heat. She took a daffodil out of the arrangement, cut an inch off the stem and replaced it, tipping her head to one side to survey the effect.

"Well, Robert's an artist, too," Marissa pointed out, "and he needs a place to work."

Robert was sorting out the contents of the bags, putting vegetables and salad greens beside the sink, bulk chocolate by the stove, and meat, butter, and cream on the top shelf of the refrigerator. He looked through all the bags again and said, "Where's the light cream for the twice-baked potatoes?"

"You just put it in the refrigerator," Marissa said.

"No, that was the heavy cream for the chocolate mousse."

"There's a difference?" Marissa said. "I thought cream was cream, and you'd goofed up and put it on the list twice."

"When it comes to cooking," Robert said, "I do not make mistakes. I experiment, yes, and sometimes my tests are less than successful. But I do not make mistakes."

"Use milk," Kim suggested.

"I might, if the milk was fresh," Robert said. "But it appears to have been stored in your refrigerator for some time. It was already past its prime when I made fettuccini almost a week ago.''

''Sorry, but I did warn you once that we don't cook around here,'' Kim said. ''But I guess if you can't do without it, I'll handle the charge of the light cream brigade.'' She checked her pockets for wallet and keys and went out. As she closed the door she heard Robert say something to Brenna about her first assignment being to melt the chocolate for the mousse.

At least I'm getting out of that job, Kim thought. *And Brenna deserves to be stuck with it.*

The nearest convenience store—unlike the supermarket where they'd gone for most of the supplies—was within easy walking distance. Kim turned up the collar of her jacket against the brisk spring breeze and sauntered along, enjoying the fresh air. On the return trip she wanted to dawdle even more, since she was feeling less than excited about returning to the apartment. But she supposed Robert would be waiting anxiously for his cream.

The elevator doors were closing as she crossed the lobby, so she called, ''Hold the elevator!'' and ran.

A hand stretched out to stop the door from closing and Tanner said, "Anxious to keep me company?"

Just my luck, Kim thought. She hadn't seen him since their conversation in his office, two full days ago. He hadn't even come around the apartment to see Brenna over the weekend. But now that they were face-to-face, she supposed he was going to want an answer. Was she going to agree to a merger...or not?

He pushed the button for Kim's floor. "How's Chris doing?"

"Fine. The catalog's moving along nicely. Aren't you awfully early for the party?"

"Brenna asked me to come to help set up the dinner table."

"Oh, yes. Since we don't own one we had to borrow a table from the party rooms downstairs. The maintenance men delivered it yesterday." She eyed him and added with only a hint of maliciousness, "I don't know why Brenna didn't have them set it up then."

"Probably a lack of space."

"No doubt. And, of course, Brenna wanted you to feel needed. To be a real part of the dinner party."

He didn't answer. He didn't have to, Kim thought; it was apparent he'd gotten the message. It didn't seem to bother him, though—if anything, he seemed entertained at the idea.

"So who's your date tonight?" he asked.

"Technically, Robert is."

"So you'll be stuck in the kitchen with him? That's not much fun. Of course, I didn't expect that you'd be inviting the guy who took you to dinner last week."

"That reminds me," Kim mused. She'd had every intention of following through on her promise to send Gregg a check for her half of their dinner, but she'd forgotten to do it.

"What really happened, anyway? Don't keep me in suspense, Kim, it's driving me crazy."

Why not tell him? she thought. Refusing would only make the episode seem bigger and more important than the reality had been. And why should she care if he thought she looked like a bit of a fool? Maybe he'd reappraise his offer to merge the companies, and then Kim wouldn't have to make a decision after all.

She looked him over appraisingly. "Would you expect a woman to go to bed with you just because you bought her dinner?"

"Is that what the jerk did? No, I wouldn't."
He seemed to consider. "Maybe if I'd bought
her two dinners, but—"

Kim glared at him.

"Oh, all right. I would only expect a woman
to go to bed with me if she made a bet to—"

"I didn't lose."

He didn't seem to be listening. "And if she
then welshed on her promise, I'd consider anything fair."

"Anything? I suppose that means I'm not
safe in the elevator with you."

"Actually you're quite safe. Elevators were
never my idea of comfort when it comes to
making love—I'm a bed man myself. Of
course, a nice soft couch will do in a pinch."
He paused thoughtfully. "Or plush carpet isn't
too bad, either. Besides, that bet was to go to
bed with me, not *go to couch,* or *go to carpet....* Come on, Kim—where's your sense of
humor?"

She tried to laugh, but all that came out was
a sort of weak croak—because she hadn't been
amused by his description, she'd been aroused.
She'd suddenly had no trouble at all picturing
Tanner lounging in a king-size bed with red

satin sheets. Or lying on a black leather couch. Or stretched out on a deep white carpet...

This is nuts, Burnham. You're losing it. Knock it off, right now.

She tried to revise the troublesome mental images by picturing him half-dressed, because there wasn't a man in the world who wouldn't look silly if he was wearing socks and a shirt and nothing else.

Except for Tanner. He looked just fine.

No—more than fine. He looked delectable.

She didn't realize that she'd actually licked her lips until she saw Tanner's gaze focus on her mouth, and then it was too late.

There was a marvelous inevitability about their coming together, in the way that their bodies met and clung, the way his arms felt, the way she automatically tipped her head back to precisely the correct angle for his kiss.

It was a perfect kiss. Neither too soft nor too firm. Not demanding, but somehow masterful— as if he had absorbed her desires and substituted his own, leaving her no free will and no thought except how to increase their mutual pleasure. She leaned into him, wanting more, and he deepened the kiss, holding her even closer.

It was a very good thing indeed that he wasn't one to make love in an elevator, she thought dimly. Because if he had been...

A shock wave hit her, and she pulled away just as the elevator swished to a stop.

What was she thinking? He had come to see Brenna, to spend the evening with her. Not Kim.

Though what was it Marissa had said? *It's not really a date for any of us....*

Well, if it wasn't a date, only a group of friends getting together for dinner, then she wasn't exactly poaching her roommate's guy. Kim supposed that should make her feel better, but somehow it didn't.

What it all boiled down to, she thought, was that Tanner was an opportunist and she was an idiot.

"Kim," he said. His voice was low and sounded as if it had been sand-papered.

She didn't look at him. "I'm sure Brenna will be waiting."

She unlocked the door and went straight to the kitchen to deliver Robert's cream. He was just sliding the beef tenderloin, now wrapped in a flaky-looking pastry, into the oven.

"Thanks," he said. "I'll get started on the potatoes right away."

Throughout the evening, she tried not to look at Tanner. But it wasn't easy, and even if she hadn't been sitting directly across the table from him she suspected he would have been like a magnet, drawing her gaze.

Her senses were on edge, more acute than ever before. The tenderloin seemed juicier, the vinaigrette tarter, the potatoes smoother than anything she had ever eaten before. But taste was only part of it. The sound seemed to have been turned up, and her vision was clearer.

Was Brenna reacting differently to Tanner than she did to her usual dates? Was she really talking more loudly, gesturing more broadly? And if so, why? Did she suspect what had happened in the elevator? Or was Kim imagining the whole thing?

Marissa helped to clear the table. Then, while Robert made coffee, she brought out the individual servings of chocolate mousse. Each of the six was beautifully swirled on top, but they were presented in small plastic tubs that had once held margarine, sour cream, or cottage cheese.

"We forgot we didn't exactly have matching stemware," Marissa said cheerfully. "It turned out to be a good thing after all that we hadn't cleaned out the refrigerator in a few months. Oh, don't look at me like that," she told Dan. "They've all been washed."

Still looking doubtful, Dan picked up his spoon and dipped it cautiously into the mousse.

Marissa sat down next to him and dug happily into her dessert. Kim watched as with the first taste Marissa's expression went from anticipation to shock to distaste. She swallowed with an obvious effort and called, "Robert, why is the mousse so bitter?"

"Because it's dark chocolate."

"But—" Marissa looked helplessly at her dish. "It tastes like there's no sugar."

"Impossible." Robert poured coffee for everyone, sat down and sampled his own mousse. Kim studied him with fascination as his expression mirrored Marissa's. "There's no sugar," he muttered.

"I thought you didn't make mistakes in the kitchen," Marissa said slyly. She dipped the very tip of her spoon into the mousse and took aim; the bit of chocolate soared across the table and splattered Robert's tie. "That's what you get for letting Brenna distract you."

Robert fired back, sending a huge spoonful of mousse into Marissa's hair. Soon Brenna, caught in the crossfire, shrieked and retaliated against them both, but her aim was poor and she hit Dan squarely in the nose.

Kim held up her napkin as a shield. Peeking over the edge to see if it was safe to come out, she found herself once more looking at Tanner. Still pristine himself, he was watching the battle with a sparkle in his eyes. Suddenly, as if he could feel her gaze, he turned and looked at her, and smiled.

Kim felt as if the world had lurched to a standstill. Her hands clenched on her napkin.

So that's what's wrong with me, she thought, with sudden, blinding clarity. It hadn't been loyalty to her roommates that had caused her such pain where Tanner was concerned. It hadn't been guilt which had nagged at her when she'd found herself attracted to him. It was jealousy. Pure and simple jealousy that he was dating Marissa and Brenna, but not her.

She had invited Tanner to the Bachelor Bazaar because she wasn't interested in him in a romantic way. But she had been wrong—so very wrong.

She wanted Tanner for herself. And she wanted him forever.

CHAPTER NINE

KIM'S overacute senses seemed to have suddenly shut down. No longer were the voices louder, the colors brighter. Instead the sounds were drawn out, as if everyone were speaking in slow motion. And everything around her looked blurry—except for Tanner. The entire world seemed to have gone out of focus, leaving only his face clear. The room no longer seemed warmer than normal, either. Instead Kim felt as if she'd been dumped abruptly into ice water by the sudden realization of what she had done.

What she had unconsciously been doing for months now. Or maybe even longer than that.

She had been falling in love with Tanner Calhoun.

She had had no hint at the time—or perhaps she simply hadn't wanted to let herself think about what was happening. Now, looking back, she could clearly see what had been going on.

Each and every time they'd come up against each other, she had felt keenly competitive and

225

sometimes a bit resentful of the superior equipment and staff that made him so hard to beat. Or at least that was what she had told herself she was feeling. In reality, she had been acutely aware of him not as a competitor, but as a man. She thought she had been concentrating only on business, but in reality it wasn't bids and jobs and profits that had threatened her. It had been the deep-down knowledge that she was intrigued by Tanner himself.

No wonder Kim had written off as a bimbo every woman she'd seen with him. She'd been convincing herself that he couldn't possibly be serious about any one of them. *Because he's waiting for me, I suppose,* she thought cynically.

She hadn't wanted to go to the school carnival with Dan. In fact, she remembered telling Marissa something about not wanting to lead him on. That much, at least, had been the truth—for somewhere deep inside, Kim had already known that no other man—not Dan, not Robert, not Gregg—could possibly fill the spot she'd reserved for Tanner.

Left to her own choices, she wouldn't have invited him to the Bachelor Bazaar at all. If questioned, she would no doubt have explained that since dating was the last thing she thought of in connection with Tanner Calhoun, the possibility of including him hadn't even popped into her mind. But that story would have been a half-truth at best. The real reason she wouldn't have invited him was much more simple. She didn't want to share him.

Not that he was hers to share—or to keep to herself, for that matter. But she would like it very much if he was.

Brenna had nagged her into inviting him, so she had done so. But even then, deep inside, Kim had known her own heart. No wonder she'd been so eager to keep him away from others at the party—not because he might tell the guys about the Bachelor Bazaar, but because he might find the other women intriguing.

As, indeed, he had. That was really no wonder, Kim thought as she glanced around the table. He had been attracted to Marissa—gentle, warmhearted, honest, genuine Marissa. And to Brenna—gorgeous, glamorous, self-assured Brenna.

Kim had been irritated when he started seeing Marissa, but not, as she'd told herself at the time, because she was afraid he'd break Marissa's heart. And she'd been outright annoyed when he'd started to hang around with Brenna—but not because she was concerned that Brenna might get hurt, or even for that matter that Marissa might be wounded because Tanner had turned away from her. All those things might happen, and Kim would regret it if anyone got hurt—but her roommates' feelings weren't uppermost in her mind.

No wonder she'd had such guilty feelings—because Kim had wanted him for herself. And so, subconsciously, she had set out to force him to notice her.

On the night of the carnival, he had invited her to dance—but the idea had been Kim's to begin with. *My toes are twitching,* she had said. Now she felt ashamed of herself. How obvious could a woman be?

Then there was the bet. That preposterous bet. Though she kept insisting that she hadn't agreed to the terms in the first place, the fact was it had been Kim who had set it up. She'd tossed out the challenge in a negative sort of way, but she'd said it nevertheless. *If you're expecting that I'll do something completely crazy like offer to sleep with you...* If she hadn't been interested in him—already thinking about sleeping with him—the idea would never have occurred to her.

And ever since then, she'd been fantasizing about that bet, and about making good on it.

There was the incident tonight in the elevator—kissing him and then trying to rationalize that it was all right as long as he wasn't seriously dating Brenna—when what had really been bothering her was the idea that he wasn't dating Kim herself.

She didn't doubt that he'd been affected by that kiss. The rough edge in his voice had made it clear that he hadn't walked away unscathed. But what had created that rasp? Dawning awareness of Kim as a desirable woman?

Yeah, right, she thought. Sheer animal arousal would be more like it. Or, most likely of all, pure terror of how she had thrown herself at him and what she might do next. Making a casual bet was one thing. Carrying through with it—especially with a woman who might take sleeping together seriously—was another thing altogether.

She had been a fool all the way through. And now that she knew it, the question was what she was going to do about it.

Behave naturally, Kim told herself. That was rule number one, and she was determined to keep it.

She reached over to Robert, cautious not to put herself between the combatants even though the room seemed to have stopped raining chocolate, and scooped a lump of mousse off his tie. "That spot should be treated right away or it'll stain," she warned.

"Why bother?" Brenna asked. She sounded a bit breathless from the battle. "That tie has blobs and splotches of every color in the rainbow already. How will anybody even be able to tell that it's stained?"

Kim privately agreed that Robert's neckwear would take the grand championship in a wild-tie contest. But he had flipped up the end of it for inspection, and he was looking a bit crestfallen. Kim wasn't sure whether his unhappiness was because of Brenna's comment or the damage done to a favorite accessory, but she didn't intend to add to the problem. "They'll know because chocolate brown isn't part of the rainbow," she shot back at Brenna. "Come on, Robert. Cold water is called for. I may not know what I'm doing in the kitchen, but put me in the laundry room and I'm dynamite."

*   *   *

The merger was out of the question now. It didn't take long, once the dinner party was over and she had a chance to think, for Kim to reach that conclusion.

Combining the companies would mean working with Tanner all the time. Even though they'd still be located in separate buildings, handling separate projects, there would no doubt be near-constant contact—and that, she knew, would be more than she could handle. Being around him…answering to him…calling him up to ask questions—it would just be too difficult to do those things, knowing that to him she was just another employee.

In fact, it was going to be difficult enough to face Tanner at the odd bid-letting—but Kim knew she'd just have to deal with that problem as it came up. She wouldn't have any option but to see him then, so she'd simply have to get used to it.

Unless, of course, she just didn't bid on the jobs she knew he'd be going after.

The sheer foolishness of that statement took a moment to sink in, but when she realized what she'd been thinking Kim was stunned. Not to go after business she wanted because it might mean confronting Tanner? She might just as well close down Printers Ink right now.

You have truly got it bad, Burnham, she told herself.

How had this happened? The only thing Kim could figure out was that it had crept up on her so slowly that there had been nothing much to notice. And, she had to admit, even when there had been something out of the ordinary, she had refused to recognize it for what it was. Even when her own feelings had been so apparent as almost to bite her in the nose, she'd denied what was really going on.

But she couldn't deny it any longer.

Not until she had concluded that the merger was impossible did she realize how much her thinking had been trending toward joining forces with Tanner, toward accepting his offer.

"Well, of course that's what you were leaning toward," she told herself irritably. "Only it wasn't entirely business you had in mind, my girl."

She obviously had no choice but to turn down the merger. But the problem was how to do that and still stay on reasonable terms with Tanner—particularly right now, with the Westway catalog only half-printed. She didn't think Tanner was the vindictive sort, but she couldn't exactly blame him if he responded to her refusal with a demand that she return her borrowed pressman instantly. Loaning staff to a prospective partner was one thing, but making it possible for a competitor to stay in business was another thing altogether.

But she couldn't just say no. She would have to give him an explanation of why she wasn't interested in the merger. Unfortunately, she absolutely couldn't tell the truth. *You see, Tanner, I'd have trouble working for a man I've fallen in love with.* If he didn't burst out laughing like a hyena, he'd turn pale and run—and either reaction would hardly leave them on speaking terms.

So she'd have to come up with a logical reason. At least she had a little time to figure it out, Kim thought with relief. He had told her to think it over—and he could scarcely expect that she'd have time for due consideration until the Westway job was finished.

Of course, that meant she'd be returning Chris and refusing Tanner's offer all at the same time. But it would be better if he thought she was a calculating, manipulative broad, delaying her answer in order to take advantage of him, than to guess what she was really feeling.

Anything would be better than letting Tanner know the truth.

The first three days that her borrowed pressman had worked at Printers Ink, he'd already been waiting on the front step when the first regular employee turned up—so finally Kim had given him a key to the building. After that, no matter what time the rest of the crew appeared, the press was already running.

On the morning after the dinner party, Kim was the first to arrive—except for Chris, of course; the moment she walked into the building she could hear the muffled roar from the back of the building. She shook her head in wry amusement at his go-getter attitude, suspecting that the real reason he was so eager to come to work was that he was anxious to get the project finished so he could return to his more comfortable berth at Calhoun and Company. She couldn't exactly blame him.

She put her briefcase on her desk and went back to the pressroom as she did every morning to check on the progress of the Westway catalog. The press was indeed running, though at something less than half-speed—but the room appeared to be empty.

Kim was startled. Though her presses were nowhere near as large or sensitive as Tanner's, any piece of complex equipment required close supervision. Things could go wrong in a moment—and Chris was obviously experienced enough to know that.

So where was he?

Visions of Rick, lying twisted in pain beside the Ripley, flashed across Kim's mind. Perhaps he had fallen behind something, just out of sight.

"Chris?" Even as she called his name, Kim knew it was a useless gesture; because of the noise of the press he'd be wearing special gear to protect his ears.

But to her surprise the door of the storage room just off the pressroom swung open and Chris popped his head out. "Oh," he said, sounding startled. "Good morning, boss."

"You heard me all the way back there?" Kim asked in disbelief.

"Yeah." He tapped an index finger against his headgear and Kim realized that he wasn't wearing Rick's but something he'd obviously brought across the street with him. "These new earmuffs just cancel out the noise of the press but let voices come through. One thing you have to say for Mr. Calhoun—he always buys the best.''

''I see. Well, you scared the daylights out of me. I thought there was something wrong. What were you doing in the storeroom, anyway?''

Chris shuffled his feet. ''Just looking.''

''For what?''

''Well…for ideas, mostly.''

''The only ideas you'll find in that room are at least twenty years old,'' Kim said dryly.

''But it's interesting. Sort of like a museum.''

''Don't make me feel any more outdated than I already do. Someday I'm going to hire a truck and take all of that junk to the dump.''

''Oh, but ma'am—you don't want to do that.''

Kim folded her arms across her chest. ''And why not?''

''Because there are some real antiques back there.''

''I hate to burst your balloon, Chris, but there's a difference between old and valuable. And nothing in that room can possibly be old enough to qualify as antique, because the building's only been here for fifty years or so.''

Chris shook his head stubbornly. ''Then somebody picked up some used equipment somewhere along the line. There's a hand-operated press back there—the kind they used in frontier days.''

Kim frowned. It had been a good ten years since she'd set foot in the storeroom, but she certainly didn't remember any frontier-aged press.

''Say,'' Chris went on. ''I'm thinking of starting up my own business someday. I'd like to get away from the rat race.''

''Better think again. You may believe working for Tanner is a rat race, but trying to keep your own business going is ten times worse.''

''But wait till you hear what I want to do. I want to go out west to one of the tourist areas— up in the Rocky Mountains, probably—and do old-style photography and printing. You know, do up the town newspaper like it was the 1880s. Print souvenir *Wanted* posters. Stuff like that.''

''That's not an easy way to make a living.''

''But I don't need much to live on,'' he said eagerly. ''If you decide to get rid of that equipment, Ms. Burnham—well, I sure couldn't afford to pay you what it's worth, but maybe we could work out a deal.''

"A percentage of your profits?" Kim said dryly. "I'll let you know if I decide to clear out that room. In the meantime, Chris—''

"I know, we've got a catalog to print.''

"And you have a cobweb in your hair,'' Kim told him gently.

Marge was just settling behind her desk when Kim came back to the office. "You're here early,'' Marge said. "Too much rich food at the dinner party?''

Not food—just too much information to digest. "You'll never believe what Chris just told me—he says the storeroom is full of antiques. But we can't have anything that old, can we?''

Marge nodded wisely. "Oh, yes, we can. Your dad bought up an old print shop once— it had been operating in downtown Chicago since well before the fire.''

Chicago before the great fire…that would qualify as the frontier, Kim supposed—at least where Chris was concerned.

"Didn't you know that's what caused the split between the partners?''

Kim frowned. "I thought it was the Ripley press that they disagreed about.''

"That was part of the package, but to get it Ben had to take all the rest as well, and that was really what caused Charles Calhoun to blow up. He couldn't understand why Ben wanted all that junk, as he called it."

"Well, as much as I hate to side with Charles Calhoun—"

Marge nodded. "He was probably right, but he was a real jerk about it. He absolutely refused to consider it an asset of the company when the partnership split—so Ben said fine, he'd pay the business back and call it his personal property. Then it became a matter of pride, I think—Ben couldn't possibly admit that it *was* junk, so it's just been sitting back there in the storeroom gathering dust ever since."

Thoughtfully Kim went into her own office and closed the door. Something was nagging at her, tugging at the back corner of her brain. Something that Tanner had said, that first day over lunch in his conference room....

She'd mentioned the Ripley press having caused the breakup, and he'd mused about family folklore and the differences in how two people explained the same event. Ben Burnham had told her the partners' disagreement had been about the Ripley. Charles Calhoun must have told his son it was about a load of old junk.

What does it matter? she asked herself. Tanner had said himself that whatever had happened between the partners wasn't important anymore. And he'd asked only about the Ripley. He hadn't even mentioned the other equipment.

But if Chris knew from a glimpse that it had value, then the possibility must have crossed Tanner's mind.

And why had Chris gone poking through the storeroom in the first place? Because he wanted a break from running the press? Kim doubted it, because no matter how early he'd arrived this morning, she must have been right behind him. He'd scarcely started work.

Or had he been looking because Tanner had told him to, to see if the really valuable equipment was still there?

Now that she thought about it, Tanner had been very cooperative about loaning her an employee. And Chris had been the most eager beaver on the block, coming to work at the crack of dawn, staying long past quitting time, even working the weekend without complaint. Was he doing it in order to get the job done?

Or so he could have a quiet look around when no one was watching?

It isn't important, Kim thought. Even if that old equipment was part of Tanner's motive in offering the merger, it wasn't going to get him anywhere, since she'd already decided to turn him down.

But the possibility stung nevertheless. He'd told her—and she'd unhesitatingly agreed—that Printers Ink didn't have enough assets for her to make a case for being a full partner. But if that old equipment truly was as valuable as Chris seemed to think...

I sure couldn't afford to pay you what it's worth, Chris had said. But what was it worth?

Aspirin, Kim told herself. She needed to stop on her lunch break and stock up on aspirin.

At midafternoon Kim was helping to collate and bind the first of the Westway catalogs when Marge came looking for her. ''Jasper Pettigrew is on the phone for you.''

Kim didn't stop feeding pages into the folding machine. ''Senior or junior?''

''I don't think he said. But he was talking so softly it was hard to hear what he was saying at all.''

"Then it was junior." Kim turned the machine off and followed Marge back to the office.

Pettigrew Junior—it was funny, but she'd never thought of him that way until she'd heard Tanner's name for him, and now she could hardly call him anything else—was almost whispering into the phone. "We're going to have another printing project coming up," he said. "I wanted to let you know right away so you could be ready."

"Jasper, I don't think there's much point in me bidding." *I hope to be working with the Pettigrews for a good long time,* Tanner had said. As long as he was taking that approach, she could hardly underbid him and still make the job worthwhile.

"I've arranged it," Jasper said impatiently.

"You've convinced your father to give me the job? Jasper, if the board of directors requires him to take bids—"

"I mean Mr. Calhoun won't be bidding again. I fixed that." A note of self-satisfaction crept into his voice. "You see, I suggested to my father that he order just half the number of annual reports that he actually needs. Then when they're delivered, he'll tell Mr. Calhoun there's an error and he'll have to reprint them all. But since the old ones aren't any good to anyone, we'll offer to recycle them, to save him the trouble of hauling them away.''

''And since it's only a very small error, you'll actually use them instead—and end up with all the copies you need for half the cost.'' The sheer audacity of it nearly took Kim's breath away.

''My father loved the idea,'' Jasper said modestly.

''I'll bet he did.'' *And you think telling me this will make me eager to bid the next job?*

''But that's not why I did it, of course. I wanted to discourage Mr. Calhoun from ever bidding for our business again.''

''I think that should do it,'' Kim managed to say.

''I'll fax the specs for the new job to you right now. They'll go out to everybody else next week—but by then you can be ahead of the game.''

You can say that again, Kim thought. *I'll be the very first to throw them in the trash.*

She put the phone down and sat still for a couple of minutes, rubbing her temples and thinking. The last thing she wanted to do just now was talk to Tanner, but she knew she had to warn him. He'd been decent to her—no, more than decent—where the Westway job was concerned, and when he'd loaned her Chris. She owed him a heads-up about the Pettigrews' plan.

Tanner was checking the proofs of the Pettigrew annual report when the receptionist phoned to tell him Kim was in the lobby. Anticipation trickled through him. He pushed the proofs aside and stood up as she was shown into his office.

She looked very solemn. That was understandable, he thought. It was a big decision to give up control of the business her father had left her—particularly under this set of circumstances.

You don't know that's what she's here about, he reminded himself. But of the half-dozen scenarios that sprang into his mind—some barely possible, some almost laughable—the merger was certainly the most likely. Still, she'd surprised him often enough that he'd learned not to make assumptions.

He gestured toward the chair across from his desk and said, "What brings you across the street this afternoon?"

"That," she said, and pointed at the Pettigrew proofs.

He was taken aback. "It's a little late to be arguing about this job. It's a done deal, Kim."

"Not as done as you think it is. You've been set up."

He listened without comment as she succinctly told him precisely what Pettigrew Senior intended to do. It was almost too much to take in, and he didn't really believe what she was saying until she told him that it was Pettigrew Junior who had originated the idea.

"He seems to have thought it up out of some misguided instinct to be my knight in shining armor," she said, and he watched as faint color rose in her cheeks.

"So the Pettigrews breed true after all," he said finally. "I didn't think the young man had that sort of cunning in him."

"Neither did I," Kim admitted.

Pure mischief made him say, "So that couldn't have been one of the things that kept him out of the Bachelor Bazaar—you feeling that he wasn't trustworthy, I mean."

She looked a little fidgety. "Jasper Pettigrew fell short on most counts."

"Hmm. I wish I could think of that as an endorsement of those of us who did make the cut, but it leaves a lot of territory open. You know, when you came in wearing that determined expression, I thought you were here to tell me that Chris wasn't working out."

"Chris is fine. He's a good worker and the catalog's moving along right on schedule. Perhaps I should warn you about something else, though."

He watched with interest as she took a deep breath and seemed to brace herself. What on earth, he wondered, was coming next?

Kim fortified herself with a deep breath. Now was her chance to find out whether he knew the secret of the storeroom. Whether he'd sent Chris to spy. Whether he had deliberately not told her what he was really after when he offered the merger.

"You may be losing him before long," she went on. "He wants to be independent, to work for himself."

"That's not an uncommon dream. Usually, after a short while, reality sets in."

Kim plunged on. "In fact, he's offered to take a lot of old equipment off my hands. Junky stuff that my dad bought years ago and stored in a back room. I'm tempted to take him up on it. Clear it all out so I can use the space."

She watched him closely, but Tanner seemed to be only mildly interested. She didn't know what she'd expected, but that wasn't it. Neither was shock, of course—she knew firsthand that Tanner could keep a poker face when he wanted to. But if Chris was acting under Tanner's instructions, surely there should have been some reaction at the idea that his spy had ideas of his own. A flicker in the eyes, perhaps, or a restless shift of his hand. But there was nothing.

"And he thinks he could be competitive, with that kind of equipment?"

And just how much do you know about exactly what kind of equipment he's trying to buy? "Well, not against you and me. But that's not the sort of business he has in mind."

"I thought when you said I might be losing him that perhaps you'd offered him a full-time job," Tanner mused.

"I doubt I could afford him. That reminds me, though—would you prefer it if I pay Chris directly, or leave him on your payroll and re-imburse you for the time he works for me?''

Tanner shrugged. ''There's no hurry about deciding. In fact, you won't need to do either one if we're going to combine forces.''

She'd known when she crossed the street that the question would inevitably come up. But now that the moment had arrived, she felt as nervous and edgy as if she'd suddenly found a ticking time bomb under her chair. Tanner had made the statement as if the merger was a fore-gone conclusion—but she couldn't let that mis-apprehension go on. She owed him a prompt response. ''We're not going to merge the com-panies, Tanner.''

He picked up a fountain pen and toyed with it, looking at the gold engraving on the barrel rather than at her. ''Is that a final answer or an invitation to make you a better offer?''

''Final,'' Kim said firmly.

''May I ask why?''

And I was thinking just today that I had lots of time to figure out a convincing reason, Kim thought. Well, she'd just have to do the best she could—cross her fingers that the story she'd come up with would do, gloss over the main points, and hope he didn't insist on details.

"It's because of my stepmother," she said. "She's the only one left who actually went through the split-up of the partnership, and she still hasn't gotten over all the bad feelings that went along with it. Reuniting the companies would be very uncomfortable for her."

Tanner's voice was level. "The last I knew your stepmother had nothing to say about Printers Ink. She inherited all of Ben's personal holdings, but the business was left entirely to you."

Kim was taken aback. Obviously he knew a lot more about the division of Ben Burnham's estate than Kim would have liked. But had she really expected anything else? Of course he'd have checked out Printers Ink before he'd offered to take it under his wing. Whatever else Tanner Calhoun might be, he was a savvy businessman.

"Letha isn't an official partner," Kim said. "But she does have a stake in the company. A personal interest." *In the bottom line, if nothing else.* "I feel I have to respect her wishes, and as long as she opposes the idea of a merger..." She shrugged. "I just can't make that kind of decision without her agreement."

"She does seem to still be fighting the feud," Tanner mused.

Kim felt her breath catch. She'd forgotten, in her haste to create a workable excuse, that Letha had admitted to talking to Tanner. But surely the woman hadn't said anything that would conflict with Kim's story—which was all true, as far as it went. Letha wouldn't even breathe the name of Calhoun, for heaven's sake.

"She never forgave your father for the split," she said. "She married half of a very profitable business, but when the partnership broke up, she suddenly had a whole lot less than half, and she blamed Charles for the sudden change in her standard of living."

"I'd think in that case she'd take satisfaction in winning out, in the end. Calhoun and Company admits that we can't do without Printers Ink after all—surely she can appreciate the irony in that?"

That was an odd way to phrase it, surely. "What do you mean, you can't do without Printers Ink?"

"You're sounding suspicious again, Kim." Tanner put the fountain pen down. "It was only a manner of speaking. If telling your step-mother that I've surrendered and admitted defeat helps to convince her, what harm does it do?''

''I don't think it would make any difference.'' *At least not to me.* Kim stood up. ''Look, Tanner, I need to get back to work. And since we seem to have finished this discussion...''

He didn't protest, merely stood and ushered her to the door.

What did you expect, Kim? she mocked herself. *A goodbye kiss?*

All in all, she thought, he'd taken it pretty well. She couldn't expect more than that.

Kim couldn't stop herself from looking back as she crossed the street, but when she saw Tanner standing by his office window she quickly turned away. Sadness swept over her— regrets, she told herself, for all the possibilities which had lain open for Printers Ink, opportunities which now would never come to pass.

Her case of the doldrums certainly wasn't personal. She wouldn't—couldn't—allow it to be.

Only when the Westway catalog was finally finished a week later was Kim able to relax a little. Jerri Wallace loved the result and immediately began talking about the next project, and Kim listened respectfully, saying she'd think it over. But though she didn't intend to burn her bridges, she didn't think she'd be bidding on Westway's next job.

Successful though the project had been, the toll it had taken on Printers Ink had been high. They were all dead tired and snappish, and now that it was safely over, Kim was aghast at the risk she'd undertaken. If it hadn't been for Tanner loaning her Chris, she couldn't have pulled it off at all. She'd been lucky this time, but she couldn't count on that happening again. It was time to get back to serious, ordinary business. Jobs like printing Tyler-Royale direct mail advertising circulars wasn't glamorous, but it paid the bills and it was steady.

Or at least it was supposed to be steady. They'd all been too busy working the catalog to worry about other business—in fact, on the few occasions when the Tyler-Royale job had crossed her mind, Kim was vaguely grateful that the circular had been delayed so they didn't have to juggle it in the midst of the rush. But once the catalog was safely in Westway's hands, she sat down to clear off her desk and take stock. There must be a hundred things waiting for her attention which had been pushed aside in the last, frantically busy week, but Tyler-Royale was at the top of the list.

The woman she usually worked with in Tyler-Royale's advertising department had never called her back, so Kim phoned again. She was on hold, waiting for the woman's assistant to find her, when Letha Burnham breezed into her office and sat down, uninvited.

Kim put a hand over the telephone. "I'm a little busy just now, Letha."

"This won't take long. I just dropped in to tell you I'm leaving for the Caribbean tomorrow."

"Going on the cruise after all? That's nice." *And how much do you want this time?*

"Now that everything's settled... That reminds me, I also came to tell you that there will be some movers coming by here to pick up some things I sold."

Kim said slowly, "What things? You don't own anything here, Letha."

"Not anymore, no." She laughed. "Good old Ben—I thought he'd left me just a bunch of junk, but it turns out to be quite valuable after all."

A bunch of junk. Kim could almost feel herself turning white. "If you're talking about the equipment in the storeroom, Letha—"

"I certainly am," Letha said coldly. "And if you're going to argue that it's yours, think again. That equipment never belonged to the partnership, so it never was part of Printers Ink. It was Ben's—and he left everything outside of the business to me."

Marge's words from just a few days ago rang hollow in Kim's head. *Ben said he'd pay the business back and call it his personal property.*

"Who bought it?" Kim asked, but she already knew the answer. There were only two people who would have been interested, only two people who knew what was in that storeroom. Chris didn't have enough money to satisfy Letha, much less to make her purr like this, so that left only one serious contender.

Besides, only Tanner knew that Ben Burnham's personal property had been left to his wife, not his daughter. And only Tanner knew that the contents of the storeroom hadn't belonged to Printers Ink, but to Ben. Only Tanner knew about Letha.

"Such a nice young man," Letha said. "Nothing at all like his father. So thoughtful. So cooperative. So *generous.*"

The phone clicked. "Kim?" said the woman she'd habitually worked with at Tyler-Royale. "I'm so sorry to have to tell you this. The decision was just made yesterday, and I argued against it, but I lost. You're not going to be getting the circular this time—and probably not the future ones, either."

Kim closed her eyes and waited for the inevitable blow.

"They're going to Calhoun and Company," the woman said. "They gave us an offer so good my boss said he couldn't possibly refuse."

CHAPTER TEN

BATTERED by the double shock, Kim could do nothing but sit frozen in her chair. Waves of words continued to rush over her—Letha gloating from just across the room, and the Tyler-Royale advertising executive apologizing profusely over the telephone—but as far as Kim was concerned, they might as well have both been speaking Martian.

Either piece of news would have been enough to knock Kim to her knees. Together, hitting her like a prizefighter delivering a one-two punch, the impact wasn't just doubled, it was multiplied.

And I was stupid enough to think he took it well, when I told him there wouldn't be a merger. What a fool she had been, just because Tanner had remained calm, not to expect something like this.

In the years since she'd come to work at Printers Ink, she had never known Tanner to lose his temper over anything. He'd even greeted the news of the Pettigrews' underhanded plot with equanimity instead of the fury it deserved.

But the fact that he never yelled or turned red in the face didn't mean that he didn't ever feel angry. And in some ways, cold and considered anger was a whole lot more menacing than any amount of shouting. Quiet anger ran deeper, and it lasted longer. And it hurt worse to be on the receiving end of it.

Especially because it was the last thing Kim had anticipated.

You thought because he was gentle with you that he'd never be anything else, a small voice in the back of her mind whispered. *But you were a fool to think that the favors he did you were anything personal.*

He'd stepped aside and handed her the Westway job, and by loaning her Chris he'd made it possible for her to succeed. But both those things had happened when he had thought the companies were going to merge. Now that he knew they weren't....

There's blood in the water, Kim thought. *And Tanner's the shark, circling for the kill.*

This time Kim didn't give the receptionist at Calhoun and Company a chance to call Tanner, or even to show her to his office. Without a word, she stormed through the atrium and down the hall with the receptionist in hot, if startled, pursuit.

As she flung open the door of his office, Tanner looked up from his desk. "I gather you'd like to see me, Kim," he said, and waved the receptionist away.

She braced her hands on the edge of his desk and looked at the paperwork scattered there. "Is this the Tyler-Royale account you stole from me?"

His eyebrows rose. "Stole is a very strong word."

"No doubt your defense is that I gave it to you. And I suppose I did, in a way. I told Jerri Wallace that day in her office that Tyler-Royale was one of my big accounts. What a fool I was, to think that because you were comparing our bids you wouldn't be listening to every word I said—and drawing conclusions."

"As a matter of fact," Tanner said mildly, "I wasn't listening. I don't remember you mentioning any particular client that day—or, for that matter, on any other day."

She stared at him in utter disbelief.

"I was invited to submit a bid for Tyler-Royale's work, and I did so—which hardly qualifies as stealing. So with that settled, what else can I do for you, Kim? Short of stabbing myself in the heart with a paper knife," he added wryly, "in case that's what you're about to suggest."

"I couldn't have phrased it better myself. Are you trying to put me out of business?"

"Careful, Kim. Asking questions like that implies that you think I could do it, and it might give me ideas."

"As if you don't have them already. I want to know what's in that storeroom. And don't ask which storeroom, because Letha told me all about the deal."

He looked her over appraisingly. "You actually don't know what's in there? You disappoint me, Kim. You could go look around far more easily than I could—it's your storeroom."

Kim didn't particularly want to admit it, but she'd done exactly that. The moment she'd finally gotten rid of Letha, she'd gone back to the storage room and to the best of her ability checked out every piece of equipment in the place. There was one corner she hadn't been able to delve into, because it was blocked by a stack of cabinets containing old hand-set type. That was as close as she got to antique—the type was collectible, but it wasn't exactly rare. Nowhere could she spot anything that hinted of more than moderate value. Finally, puzzled, she had given up. What on earth was worth the amount of money Letha said he'd paid her? Had Tanner simply guessed wrong? Had Chris misled him? Or had Kim missed something?

"I've looked," she admitted, "and as far as I can tell it's nothing more than a pile of junk. Worth a few dollars as scrap, perhaps. So what's so valuable that you'd pay Letha an arm and a leg to get hold of it?"

"Since it's not your junk," Tanner said, "it really isn't your business what I bought, or how much I paid for it. But since you've asked me so nicely..." There was an expectant pause.

Kim gritted her teeth. "All right. Will you *please* tell me what in that room is so valuable?"

"Nothing," Tanner said softly. "Nothing at all."

"You can't honestly expect me to believe that, Tanner."

"It's the truth. Because it wasn't really the equipment I bought at all. I was buying Letha's cooperation."

Kim stared at him, speechless.

"You told me she opposed the idea of a merger," Tanner went on. "Now she doesn't."

"You bought a truckload of junk—for what even Letha admitted was a very generous amount of money—because she stood in the way of the merger?" Even to her own ears, Kim's voice sounded shrill.

"From the way you described her," Tanner mused, "she didn't seem like the type who would understand the concept of goodwill, and I figured if I told her what I was really after, she'd have held out until hell froze. So I offered to buy Ben's old equipment instead. Turning junk into cash is something she clearly understood."

"Letha would," Kim admitted. "Especially if she didn't have to get her hands dirty in order to collect."

"But after cutting the deal she did, she can't possibly oppose you making an agreement of your own. So the way is now clear to combine the companies."

Even in the midst of her fury, it hadn't occurred to Kim that the situation could get even
worse—but now it had. Tanner had very neatly
spiked her guns by knocking the foundations
out from under her reasons for refusing the
merger.

So she could either agree to it, or she could
come up with a whole new set of reasons to
explain why she wouldn't. Neither option
looked like a promising move.

For one thing, all her old objections still
held—much as she wanted to agree, she simply
couldn't stand working with him on a daily ba-
sis, caring about him as she did. And any new
reason she gave would be immediately suspect,
because if it was so important an objection
now, why hadn't she brought it up at all in the
first discussion?

Of course, whispered a little voice at the back
of her brain, she could still tell him the truth....

One thing was guaranteed about that course
of action, Kim thought. If she was to confide
exactly why she couldn't ever work with him,
she'd never have to deal with the subject again.
She'd have to endure a couple of minutes of
heartrending embarrassment and shame as she

confessed her guilty secret, but Tanner would never again renew the offer.

But it wouldn't really be a long-term solution. Every time she saw him, she would feel that pain all over again. Not the pain of loving him—she'd have to deal with that every day no matter what she did now—but the pain of knowing that he understood in minutest detail exactly how foolish she had been. Every time they both attended a bid-letting or a Chamber of Commerce event…every time he came to the apartment to see Brenna or Marissa…every time he looked at Kim…

No. She could absolutely not bear that. The situation would be difficult enough as it was. To tell him any more would not only be masochistic but it would make her look pathetic—as if she hoped beyond hope that simply telling him how she felt would make him want her after all.

"The way is clear," Tanner repeated. "So how about it, Kim?"

"No." She scarcely recognized her own voice.

"Perhaps you should talk to Letha again before you answer."

"I don't need to. The answer is no."

"Why?"

"I don't have to give you my reasons, Tanner." She stood up.

"No, you don't have to justify it to me," he agreed. "But if you're turning this down because you still hold a grudge over what happened between my father and yours—"

Kim opened her mouth to deny it, but she stopped herself in the nick of time. What difference did it make what he thought? Believing she still nursed that old resentment would be a great deal better than having him wonder too much about what was really going on.

He was watching her, eyes narrowed. "Just one thing, Kim. You don't have to tell me the truth. But you'd be wise not to lie to yourself."

Kim watched as the goldfish swam aimless circles around the tank, and thought of the day that Tanner had brought them and stocked the aquarium. How much easier her life had seemed back then—before she had realized how important he was to her. But would she really trade her self-knowledge, painful though it could be, for the naiveté of a few weeks ago?

"You've been awfully quiet, the last few days," Marissa said.

Kim jumped, startled because she'd forgotten Marissa was even in the room. "I was just thinking."

Marissa put the cap back on her bottle of pale-pink nail polish. She didn't meet Kim's eyes as she asked, "Have you seen Tanner lately?"

She sounded almost plaintive, Kim thought, as if she was longing for news. And no wonder—Tanner not only hadn't called Marissa again, but he'd stopped coming around to see Brenna as well. "I'm so sorry, Riss."

"For what?" Marissa sounded genuinely puzzled.

"For introducing you to him. No, more than that. I'm sorry I thought of the damned Bachelor Bazaar in the first place. The whole thing's been nothing but a disaster."

"I wouldn't go that far, Kim."

"But look at us! You're spending the evening doing your nails. Brenna's shut in her bedroom where she says she's practicing yoga and I'm watching the goldfish. We're no better off than the night we figured out the phone bill."

"You got one out of three," Marissa mused. "That isn't bad. And by the way, you still haven't answered my question."

"About whether I've seen Tanner? Only from across the street, getting out of his car. I haven't talked to him, so I can't tell you how he's getting along. Riss, I really am sorry I got you involved with him in the first place."

Marissa shrugged. "No need to apologize for that. It was never me he was interested in anyway."

It was some relief to know that Marissa was being realistic, though Kim wasn't so certain that she was telling the absolute truth. It must have hurt when Tanner had dropped her for Brenna. "I'm glad you're taking it that way, but—"

Marissa appeared not to notice the interruption. "It was you."

The announcement hit Kim with the weight of a bucket of concrete. Was it possible that Marissa was right? That Tanner had actually been interested in Kim herself? *Darned funny way to show it,* she thought. "Oh, yeah? And how do you explain him dating Brenna?"

"Same thing. Both of us gave him an excuse to hang around here—so he could see you."

Obviously Marissa had misinterpreted things, Kim thought. But in a roundabout way, there was some sense to what she believed. Tanner *had* been interested in Kim—only it had been because of business. He'd been working toward the merger even before Kim had invented the Bachelor Bazaar; the day he'd invited her to coffee had been the opening gambit in the deal. No doubt he'd seen the bazaar as a handy way to further his own interests.

"That still doesn't explain why he was dating both of you," Kim said.

"Oh, that was my idea. I knew you were far too loyal to swipe a man from a friend. Still, if he was always there, but obviously not attached to anyone in particular, you'd be more likely to see him as he really is." The telephone rang at her elbow and she picked it up, careful not to mar her nail polish.

Kim shook her head in disbelief. "You're a hopeless romantic, Marissa."

"Just a sec, Dan." Marissa cupped her hand over the mouthpiece and smiled at Kim. "Of course I'm a hopeless romantic. What else could I possibly be?"

"A sensible romantic would make a nice change," Kim said. "I haven't talked to Dan in a week, and I thought he'd given up. Do me a favor, Riss—if he's looking for me, tell him I'm not here."

"He's not looking for you. And by the way, don't write off the Bachelor Bazaar as a total failure."

"Why not?"

"You may have nothing better to do than watch the goldfish tonight. But Brenna's not in her bedroom contemplating her navel, she's exercising so she can eat whatever marvelous gooey dish Robert's planning to cook for her this weekend. And I'm manicuring my nails because Dan's taking me up to Wisconsin as soon as school's out tomorrow—so I can meet his parents."

After one brief glance at Jasper Pettigrew's fax, Kim had ignored the specifications for Pettigrew Senior's next printing job. But on the afternoon when the bids were due, she found herself leafing through the specs and wondering how Tanner had handled the Pettigrews' scheme. Not that she'd likely ever find out.

She tossed the packet toward the wastebasket and tried to focus on her own work. But she couldn't get Marissa's words out of her mind.

It was never me he was interested in, Marissa had said. *It was you.* And no doubt that was true—as far as it went. Tanner had been interested in Kim, but only because she was such an important part of Printers Ink.

Marissa, however, hadn't stopped there. Her interpretation was understandable, Kim told herself. Show a hopeless romantic an encounter—any kind of encounter—between a man and a woman, and she'd make it into a love story even if she had to twist the people involved into pretzels to make it believable. Kim didn't even want to think what kind of interpretation Marissa could create if she knew about that kiss in the elevator. Or, for that matter, the silly bet. Not that either of those things had meant anything, of course.

In fact, it was beyond foolish even to think about Marissa's convictions—but that didn't stop Kim from doing it.

Exactly what had Tanner meant, as she was walking out of his office that last time, when he'd told her that she'd be wise not to lie to herself? He'd said something about her holding a grudge, but then his eyes had narrowed as if a new suspicion had risen in his mind. As if he might have seen the truth, or at least suspected how she felt about him.

Marge called, ''The Pettigrew person's on the phone for you again, Kim,'' and Kim pushed aside her musings and answered the call.

"Where *are* you?" Jasper Pettigrew whispered. "The bids are due at three o'clock, and only one has come in yet. I know you all like to leave these things to the last minute so there's no chance somebody can cheat by getting a glimpse of the other bids, but this is pushing it, Ms. Burnham."

So that's how Tanner fixed Pettigrew Senior, Kim thought. *By passing the word so nobody's willing to work with him.* She had to admit it was effective, but somehow she'd expected something more subtle from Tanner.

She shifted the phone to her other hand and picked up her pen again. "If you've gotten one bid, Jasper, I'd advise your father to consider himself lucky and take it. Goodbye."

"But it's from Calhoun!" Jasper howled. "And the whole idea was to keep him from bidding against you!"

Kim was puzzled. "Tanner actually bid the job?"

"That's what I'm trying to tell you. If you don't get over here, he'll walk off with the work."

I can't imagine that he wants it, Kim thought. Unless—was it possible that he hadn't believed her? That he thought she'd made up some kind of fairy tale about the Pettigrews so she wouldn't have to compete with him for future jobs? If Pettigrew Senior had been smart enough to hold off on finding some elusive error in his annual report...

I can't let Tanner think I did it on purpose, Kim told herself. *And I can't let him put himself at risk of another bad job. Not if I can do anything to prevent it.*

''Have you opened his bid yet, Jasper?''

''Of course not. He hasn't officially turned it in, he's just sitting here waiting for the clock to strike three. I wouldn't be surprised if he has a couple of different ones in his pocket, and he's waiting to see if there's any competition before he decides which one to give us.''

Kim looked at her watch, grabbed her jacket and dashed to catch the next train. It seemed to take forever to pull into the platform and longer yet to get to the Pettigrew plant.

When she pushed the door open and hurried down the hallway to Pettigrew Senior's office, it was barely five minutes to three and Kim was out of breath, because she'd run from the platform across the length of the parking lot.

Tanner was sitting in the tiny waiting room outside Pettigrew Senior's door, thumbing through the latest issue of a financial magazine, when Kim dropped into the seat beside him.

He gave her no more than a fleeting glance. "I wondered if you'd be here. Cutting it a little fine, I'd say."

She didn't bother to answer. "You didn't believe me, did you—about how they were planning to get their annual report for half-price? Did you think I was making up a story to leave the field clear for me to grab their business back?"

Tanner turned a page. "Of course I believed you."

Kim choked on the breath she had started to draw in order to continue her tirade, and she started to cough.

Tanner waited patiently for her to recover. When she sank back in her chair, almost limp, he said, "Kim—surely you didn't rush all the way out here to rescue me."

"Of course not," she snapped.

"Then I assume you have a bid to submit."

"Do you think I'm a fool? Why would I want to do business with these people?"

His voice dropped to an intimate whisper. "Then—if you aren't bidding and you didn't come to save me—why are you here?"

It was a very good question, one for which she had no answer. Kim considered taking refuge in another attack of coughing, but she didn't think she could get by with it. If only she had taken a single minute to think before flying off the handle like that and rushing after him.... Why must she always jump to conclusions?

She went on the offensive instead. "So what are *you* doing here? Business must be pretty tough to get these days if you actually want this job."

"Well, I had been hoping to arrange a merger that would pull me out of the shadow of bankruptcy," Tanner said calmly.

"Do, please, be serious. Printers Ink's receivables for the year wouldn't keep you going for more than a few days."

"But since that didn't work out, I've had to look for other sources of... What do you *think* I'm doing here, Kim? I'm making sure that whoever wins this bid knows who they're dealing with.''

Then he truly had believed her. Relief surged through Kim, and she relaxed.

Tanner shut the magazine with a snap and said, ''Come on. It's past three and nobody's going to show up now. Let's get out of here.''

She could hardly plead that she wanted to stick around and socialize with the Pettigrews. And it made no sense whatsoever to insist on riding the train back, when Tanner would be driving right by Printers Ink. She was stuck.

Next time, Kim told herself, *stop and think!*

She tried to ignore the expression of shocked horror on Jasper Pettigrew's face when they passed his office cubicle together.

As she settled into the passenger seat of Tanner's Mercedes, Kim realized that he couldn't ask uncomfortable questions as long as she was controlling the conversation. So she said brightly, ''I'm dying of curiosity. How did you handle the problem with the annual report?''

''I called up Pettigrew Senior and told him I'd been studying his net-profit numbers and I couldn't understand how a company as successful as his could possibly have so few stockholders." Tanner waited for traffic to clear and pulled out of the parking lot.

Kim frowned. "I don't see why that would force him to admit he'd ordered the wrong number of reports."

"I suppose it didn't hurt when I implied that I was willing to invest in such a profitable company myself, if he could convince me that there were more than just a few stockholders to share the risk."

"So he actually confessed to the correct number?"

Tanner shrugged. "I suspect it was either that or admit that he's been cooking the books to make the company look more profitable than it actually is. I got my money, so I don't really care which it was." He cast a look sideways at her. "How are the girls?"

"Brenna and Marissa, you mean? They're not pining over you, if that's what you're hoping."

"Let me guess. Marissa's seeing Dan pretty steadily, and Brenna's racking up a string of stockbrokers."

"Half right. How did you know about Marissa?"

"You warned me yourself, after the carnival. Remember? You said Dan was acting very protective of her and I should watch out for him. What about Brenna? No stockbrokers?"

"It seems Robert's only been calling me because he was too chicken to ask for Brenna. And she admitted very calmly this morning that she's gained three pounds since he's been hanging around."

"And she isn't making a fuss about it? Now that is definitely true love."

None of the news seemed to bother him, Kim thought—but then, she'd never believed Tanner was truly serious about either Marissa or Brenna. It didn't necessarily follow, however, that he was serious about anyone else instead.

Namely you, Burnham. So don't you forget it.

The car swung into the industrial park. "Thanks for the ride," Kim said, and tried not to think about how this might be the last time she would say that.

However, instead of pulling up in front of Printers Ink, Tanner drove around the side of the building and parked the Mercedes next to Marge's Volkswagen.

Kim tried to make light of it. "Remember, Tanner? We didn't do the merger. You still work over *there.*" She pointed across the street.

"I couldn't possibly go back to work right now," he said. "Not when I'm—as you put it so well just a few minutes ago—dying of curiosity."

Kim bit her lip and didn't answer.

He helped her out of the car and took her arm with a proprietary air. Inside he closed the door of her office and leaned against it. "Aren't you going to ask what I'm so curious about?"

Kim draped her jacket over the back of a chair with far more concern than she usually showed. "I figured you'd tell me if you wanted me to know."

"That would be the first time you ever hesitated when it came to demanding cooperation," he mused. "But yes, I'll tell you what it is I'm wondering about. Why did you rush out to save me, Kim?"

"I told you, I didn't."

He smiled. "You're a terribly unconvincing liar, you know."

"And you're a..." Suddenly the need to know—to understand—welled up inside her until it threatened to drown her. "Tanner," she whispered. "Why do you want the merger?"

His voice was steady. "Because it would be good for both businesses."

"I see." She sighed. *Hope dies hard,* she told herself. *But I think that finally did it.* And perhaps it was just as well. It hurt, but at least she wouldn't be fooling herself anymore.

"And it would be good for us," Tanner said softly, "to cooperate for a change, instead of competing." Slowly he was moving closer. "We might even grow to like it."

Kim stood her ground. Just how far would he go, to get what he wanted?

And how far would she let him go? How much would it take to crush her dream, finally and completely?

"How badly do you want this merger?" Despite her best efforts to keep it steady, her voice cracked.

Tanner paused. "Of course what you're really asking is if I want it badly enough to make love to you."

The cool, almost clinical, dissection of motive made Kim feel shriveled inside. "I suppose that's what I want to know, yes."

"Then the answer is no, Kim."

She was relieved. Or at least she would be when she had a chance to think it over, she told herself. And it was utterly crazy to feel disappointed and confused in the meantime.

Suddenly he cupped her face in his hands and bent his head till his lips met hers. Kim had no time to think, to consider—only to react. It was a long, slow, sensual kiss, and it left her shivering almost painfully, as if she had been caught in a blizzard without so much as a sweater for protection.

He ended the kiss, but he didn't let go. His fingertips lay along the line of her jaw, exerting not even an ounce of pressure but yet somehow making it impossible for her to move.

She tried to pull herself together. "You want to try that one again?"

There was a mischievous glow in Tanner's eyes. "You mean the kiss, or the explanation?"

The kiss, of course. "The explanation," she said dryly. "First you say the merger isn't important enough to make you do something you don't want to, and then you start doing it anyway."

"I never said I didn't want to make love to you. In fact, I thought I'd made it pretty clear that I did want to."

She was at a loss for a moment before her brain cleared. "If you're talking about that bet—well, I never took that seriously."

"Didn't you? I did. In fact, I'll offer you a chance to go double or nothing," Tanner said cheerfully, "just as soon as I find a proposition I absolutely can't lose." He sobered. "The merger is a damn good idea, Kim, for all the reasons I gave you. There's just one little hitch. Those weren't my real reasons. At least, they weren't the important reasons."

She pulled back, staring up at him with a frown.

"I wanted to clear up the feud, get it behind us—because I hoped that, if we started working together, perhaps you could finally see me as something more than a competitor."

Her heartbeat was thudding painfully in her ears. Could he possibly mean what it sounded like he was saying?

"Because I certainly saw you as more than a competitor," he said softly. "I saw a beautiful, feisty woman that I wanted to know better. Only you wouldn't let me get close enough to do that."

I was afraid, she thought. *Too afraid of getting hurt to take a chance.*

"Then you came up with your crazy Bachelor Bazaar, and you tried your best to give me away to anyone who'd take me off your hands. So I thought, why not? With all those nice women to choose from, why be a masochist and devote myself to the one who only wanted to get rid of me? But Marissa saw through me, and she offered to help."

Kim wet her lips. "Help you—what?" she whispered.

"Help to make you see me. *Me,* not just the guy who took a job away from you now and then. She thought the merger was a silly idea, but she was convinced if you saw me up close, dating women you knew..."

"That I'd decide I wanted you myself?"

"That was the general idea."

"You used my friends to manipulate me."

"They volunteered," he said defensively. "Kim—look, I'm sorry. I suppose it was an underhanded thing to do—"

"She was right."

"—And I apologize for— *What did you say?*"

"Marissa was right," Kim said softly. "I didn't want to see it. I tried to pretend it wasn't happening. But every time I saw you with another woman, I was unhappy. And every time I went out with a man, he couldn't measure up.''

He took a deep breath, released it and pulled her close, holding her as if he'd never let her go again. As the heat of his embrace soaked deep into her bones, Kim felt warm for the first time since he'd kissed her and given her the shivers.

''You did a darn good job of hiding it,'' he said. ''When you turned down the merger offer for the second time, but you wouldn't give any reasons, I thought maybe it was because you couldn't stand me.''

She shook her head. ''No. Not that. Never that.''

''Until today. You gave yourself away a bit, you know.''

''You could have told me what you were doing out there,'' she grumbled.

''And missed out on the vision of you rushing in to rescue me from my own folly?'' He shook his head. ''I wouldn't have passed that by for the world. Such enthusiasm....''

Kim leaned back in his arms. ''As long as we're speaking of enthusiasm, did you have to throw yourself into the part with quite so much zeal? After the dinner party, when Brenna walked you to the elevator, she came back glowing like a bride.''

Tanner gave a roar of laughter. ''And you thought it was because I was kissing her out there?''

''Well, you are pretty good in an elevator,'' Kim admitted.

''No, sweetheart. She was glowing because I'd just given her the business card of a friend of mine—who happened to be searching for an advertising model who's just Brenna's type.''

''Oh. Well, since it's Brenna—that figures.''

''Robert will have his hands full with her,'' Tanner mused. ''He's a braver man than I thought.'' He kissed her long and hard, and when he let her go he said unsteadily, ''I think I told you I wasn't much for making love in nontraditional places. But keep this up and I could become a desk man, Kim.''

Kim smiled. ''I wouldn't want to be responsible for upsetting tradition—''

''Good. Then you'll marry me.''

''—so perhaps you should just remove yourself from temptation. Go back across the street to work.''

"I like my interpretation of tradition a lot better than yours." He rubbed his cheek against her hair. "Are you ever going to tell me what the rules were for choosing a bachelor for the bazaar?"

Kim shook her head. "Since you're not going to be eligible anymore, you don't need to know."

"Stubborn female," he said. "All right then, I want a promise that you won't be trading things with your girlfriends anymore."

"Anything at all? That's no fun. How about if I promise I won't trade anything except sexy lingerie?"

Tanner sounded intrigued. "What are you going to call it?"

"How about the Naughty Nighty Exchange?"

"I think that's allowed."

"Good," she said. "Because I wouldn't want you to be bored."

"I couldn't possibly be," he whispered. "The Bachelor Bazaar. The Naughty Nighty Exchange… I'll spend my life wondering what comes next."

"You'll have to wait and see." And Kim was smiling as he kissed her.

MILLS & BOON® PUBLISH EIGHT LARGE PRINT TITLES A MONTH. THESE ARE THE EIGHT TITLES FOR JULY 2003

❧

THE BLIND-DATE BRIDE
Emma Darcy

KEIR O'CONNELL'S MISTRESS
Sandra Marton

BACK IN THE BOSS'S BED
Sharon Kendrick

THE SPANIARD'S WOMAN
Diana Hamilton

AN ACCIDENTAL ENGAGEMENT
Jessica Steele

THE MARRIAGE MARKET
Leigh Michaels

ALMOST MARRIED
Darcy Maguire

THE TYCOON PRINCE
Barbara McMahon

MILLS & BOON®

Live the emotion

0603 Rom LP

MILLS & BOON® PUBLISH EIGHT LARGE PRINT TITLES A MONTH. THESE ARE THE EIGHT TITLES FOR AUGUST 2003

❧

THE PREGNANCY PROPOSAL
Helen Bianchin

ALEJANDRO'S REVENGE
Anne Mather

MARCO'S PRIDE
Jane Porter

CITY CINDERELLA
Catherine George

RUSH TO THE ALTAR
Rebecca Winters

THE VENETIAN PLAYBOY'S BRIDE
Lucy Gordon

HER SECRET MILLIONAIRE
Jodi Dawson

A WEDDING AT WINDAROO
Barbara Hannay

MILLS & BOON®

Live the emotion

0703 Rom LP